Shadows Left Behind

Ghosts, Romance, and Basketball on the Nez Perce

Indian Reservation

By Scott Wilson

This book is dedicated to Mark Wilson, from his *'ácqa*[1].

---

[1] ƏTS\kƏ: *a male's younger brother*

Preface

Most of the names in *Shadows Left Behind* are fictional. The people are real. If you ever lived in Lapwai, Idaho, you might recognize some of them. 'Milly Lawyer' is based on my friend and neighbor Mylie Lawyer, a descendent of Corbett Lawyer, Archie Lawyer, The Lawyer (*Hallalhotsoot*, a Nez Perce leader from 1847 to 1870), and Twisted Hair (*Walamottinin*, who befriended Lewis and Clark along the Clearwater River).

The spellings of Nez Perce words in *Shadows Left Behind* (except in "When the Roll Is Called Up Yonder" in Chapter Five) follow an orthographic system initially developed by linguist Haruo Aoki that reflects the nuances of the spoken language. Respellings appear in footnotes and in the glossary in the back of the book (followed by a pronunciation guide). They represent what I heard growing up. Audio pronunciations of some words are available on the Nez Perce Language Program's app.

Enit is derived from "Ain't it?" and is common in many Native American communities. *Chize* is slang for "Wow!" and is original to Lapwai High School in the 1970's.

I borrowed the photograph shown at the beginning of Part One from my 1970-1971 basketball season to show what the team in *Shadows Left Behind* might have looked like. I'm number 43.

Scott Wilson

December 31, 2016

CAST OF CHARACTERS

KEEPERS OF THE KNIFE

May

Milly Lawyer

Sam "Redwing"/"Counts" Evans

Jessica "Pretty Hair"/*Sayáq'ic húukux* Whitehawk

THE LAPWAI WILDCATS BASKETBALL TEAM

Coach Ray McNeese	Coach Earl Guerreros
Sam Evans	Luke "Lootz" Woods
Mike McNeese	Denny Smith, Jr.
Billy White	Robert "Sonny" Reuben
Jesse Waters	Terry Gibson
Larry "Junior" Sams	Jimmy Redjacket

THE GIRLS

Vicky Smith	Julia Reuben

FAMILY MEMBERS

Jeff Evans	Carol Evans
Beatrice Roberts	Gordy Roberts
Dennis Smith, Sr.	Cindy Smith
Josiah Whitehawk	Ida Whitehawk

LATAH VALLEY CHARACTERS

Ron Harper, Jr.	Ron Harper, Sr.
Lorraine Harper	Nick Yochum
Justin Murphy	Rusty Bush
Coach Roy Bradley	Co-Op Manager Clint

HISTORICAL CHARACTERS

Eliza Spalding

Suzie/Pretty Hair/*Sayáq'ic húukux*

LAPWAI SCHOOL PERSONNEL

Mrs. Preston

Reverend Matthews

Carl Richardson

Mr. Barrett

Mr. Turner

NEZ PERCE VETERANS HONOR GUARD

Melvin Highmoon

Herman Highmoon

James Redheart

Harold Moffett

SUPPORTING CAST

Travis Wheatley — State Semi-Finals Opponent

Tony Jackson — Nez Perce Nation Basketball Player from Lewiston

Harriet Whitebird — Traditional Nez Perce Cook

Silas Moses — Warm Springs Pow-Wow Master of Ceremonies

Edith Blackwolf — Jessica's Aunt in Warm Springs

Mrs. Arthur Blackeagle

PROLOGUE

The Knife

1

March 1911

May felt the icy water reach the top of her ugly white-man boots. She watched blue-tinted ice float down the Clearwater River, broken away in the spring thaw from deep, still eddies upstream, and took another step toward the swift current. "I'm not staying here anymore," she thought. "I'm going home."

May stopped. She spotted a rowboat tied to a willow tree across the river and imagined it taking her down the Clearwater, the Snake, and finally, the Columbia.

She saw herself drifting past the craggy river-canyon bluffs that cut across north central Idaho and southeastern Washington. Rock formations of wind-shaped animal figures look down on May. She knows their stories, legends of the Plateau People kept alive since ancient times. Sage-green tufts of bunch grass, prickly pear, and rabbit brush blanket the canyon draws. A few stunted pine trees jut from moss-covered crevices, catching just enough spring water or rainfall to survive. In spring, tiny yellow and white wildflowers burst into color in the few weeks between snow-melt and the too-hot, too-soon early summer suns that turn the hillsides amber-brown. It's a place where the hills show their bones.

At Celilo Falls, her father, or an uncle, or one of her brothers glimpses a battered craft wedged between two boulders along the shore upriver. He puts down his dip net and watches the spring-run salmon leap into the crashing waters a moment before climbing down the lodgepole pine scaffold clinging to the cliffs to inspect. He finds a teenage girl inside, fast asleep.

"It's May!" he shouts. He carries her to Grandfather's cabin, tiny and warm from an ever-burning stove fire, camas roots drying on the kitchen counter. Grandfather looks up from mending his gill net, smiles, and simply says, "I knew you'd come home." On the river, with her family around her, May can breathe strong again.

She doesn't have to die in Idaho of tuberculosis.

A touch on her shoulder startled May from her daydream.

"May! Let's go back, enit?"

May turned toward her friend Milly. When she first arrived at the Fort Lapwai Tuberculosis Sanatorium two months earlier on the train from The Dalles, May had told Milly that one of her grandmothers was Nez Perce. "Like you," she grinned. "So maybe we're cousins, enit?" Milly's oval face had reminded May of her sisters back home on the Warm Springs Reservation, digging roots on warm spring days on the prairie.

Milly stood by her father Corbett Lawyer on the Lapwai depot platform the day May arrived awaiting the next trainload of sick children. In those changing times, Milly understood her family's calling. Her great-grandfather, The Lawyer, was a chief. Her grandfather, Reverend Archie Lawyer, a minister. Her father was a tribal police officer, and he always found time for the homesick children at the sanatorium. Milly and he promised each other the year before to greet every frightened child coming to the TB hospital with a comforting smile and gentle embrace. Her service.

The rumble of an approaching train shook the earth, and Milly spun just in time to see the locomotive appear from behind the grain elevators. As it slowed, carloads of forlorn children neared the last leg of their journey.

As Milly started to sadly turn away, a very different scene unfolded in the railroad car stopped directly in front of her. She was surprised to see laughing children clustered around a teenage girl telling a story. A toddler bounced on the storyteller's lap. Her yarn unfolded as she became one character after another. At last, a beautiful smile spread across her face when the children realized how Coyote had again tricked his enemies.

A kind, middle-aged white woman, an Indian Health Service matron, led the children back to their seats to retrieve the cloth bags holding their few belongings. She patted the storyteller's arm and wiped away a tear. After they left her train, she would never see these children again. But by some miracle, one of them had brought a few moments of joy to everyone around her.

Milly watched the girl force a smile and descend the train's metal grate steps into an unknown future. From that moment, watching May help the others briefly forget their illnesses and then, when she thought no one could see, put on a brave face for their sakes, Milly knew she was looking at the best friend she would ever have.

And now, just as May wandered toward the river, Milly saw the sorrow in her friend's eyes. She followed and watched the longing for home pull May into the river's freezing grip. May took Milly's hand, and they returned to the picnic. Though Milly reached May just in time, she would never mention anything to May about the river.

May and Milly rejoined the others finishing their picnic lunches. Some of the stronger children rolled down the mill trace banks and ran down the slough left from the days of the Spalding Mission. Sanatorium nurses tended children too ill to play. This three-mile outing to Spalding Park had become an annual event. The first buttercups of spring offered hope.

May was still thinking of home. She reached into her dress pocket and felt for a very special gift from her brother: a double blade Barlow knife.

"You keep it, May, and it'll be our fishin' knife when you get better and bring it home. But don't let any white people see it... They'll think you're gonna scalp 'em, enit?" he joked.

But as Milly and May joined the others playing in the mill trace, May forgot about the knife. It slipped from her dress pocket as she rolled down the bank, but luckily landed near Milly's hand. Milly shoved it into her own pocket before it could be seen by a nurse. Milly would talk secretly with May later about finding a hiding place for the knife.

Milly did not have tuberculosis, so she did not live at the sanatorium. She lived in the village with her family, and Milly loved to go with her father on his rounds in his green pickup. Milly spent many hours with the children there. She would find a good place for May's knife until May was ready to go home.

One Month Later

"May!" Milly whispered urgently. "The rocks are hot. *Háamt'ic[2]!* Hurry!"

May raised her head from her pillow and looked around the room at the other girls, still asleep. Their endless coughing betrayed the girls' poisoned lungs. She turned toward the low, open window

---

[2] HƏM\tits

where Milly stood outside. Even in chilly early spring evenings, fresh night air wafted through the many windows of the Fort Lapwai Tuberculosis Sanatorium. In moments, May squeezed through the nearest window and stood outside.

"Let's go!" Milly repeated.

"Where?" May asked, bewildered.

"I'll show you," Milly beamed as she grabbed May's hand. They scurried toward the hillside beyond the many buildings serving the several hundred young TB patients there.

Tuberculosis rampaged across the reservations at the turn of the twentieth century. Stale air had nowhere to escape in these new houses. No longer could the People easily move their homes with the seasons. The whites' cattle drove away the game and trampled the fields where the best camas roots grew. It was a new world, full of disease, and Indian teens were hit the hardest.

"I'm so cold..." May shivered.

"I know...let's go! Quick!" Milly pulled her companion across the open field and into a large barn. They were welcomed by the reassuring lowing of the sanatorium's herd of dairy cows and felt their radiant warmth. May and Milly made their way in the pitch black from stall to stall, touching the backs of the gentle creatures as their eyes adjusted to the dark. Still holding each other's hand, they neared the far end of the barn and could finally see a sliver of moonlight through the slats of the barn's large double doors. Milly led May to a stack of wool blankets used during calving season.

"Here," Milly whispered as she handed May the top blanket. "You can put this around you." In the light of a full moon and with new warmth, May and Milly scampered past the sheds and smaller barns to the edge of the hospital grounds. Milly helped May over a rise at the bottom of the hill, and soon they were hidden from view, for the moment lost in their own world, free from disease and sadness.

May knew where they were: inside the long-abandoned canal used to transport spring water to the village that traversed the valley's western hills. She had heard stories from homesick children from the village who hid in the canal when they snuck out to spend a few precious hours with their families.

Milly guided May over wind fallen debris, beneath low-lying branches, and past limbs Milly held aside for her. In the hollow-darkness of the canal, May faithfully trailed her trusted friend.

"We're here!" Milly finally exclaimed. A jumble of interwoven branches blocked their way. Milly knelt and searched the ground. "Here it is!" She lifted a corner of a dark brown blanket the color of bark to reveal a tiny room. Heated rocks carefully stacked in a shallow pit glowed red. May smiled at the sight of a chipped white tin cup with tiny hand-painted blue flowers filled with water: her Christmas present to Milly. She wore the beaded barrette from Milly.

"It was all I had to give," May remembered.

Milly helped May fold her heavy blanket. "I don't think they'll miss a few of these," she confessed. On either side of the glowing stones lay more blankets, 'borrowed' from the dairy barn, covering the earthen floor.

May knew what to do. She hung her nightgown on a branch protruding from the curved wall of the sweathouse, stooped through the passageway, sat on her blanket seat, and sprinkled water on the rocks. Instantly, steam rose.

"How did you...?" May stared in amazement at the structure. Rusty tin-roof sheets lay across beams of bark-stripped poles. Here and there, starlight found its way through layers of branch camouflage and old nail holes in the tin. Milly spent the last month building this sweathouse for her best friend.

"Did your...?" May started to ask.

"Yes, he knew. I think Dad would've helped if I asked him. I would slip out really late at night to collect material. One night I felt someone watching me." Milly recalled what happened the next day.

"Milly, would you go out back with me for a minute?" Corbett Lawyer asked. When they got to the alley behind their house, he pointed to his woodpile. "I don't need so many of these tepee poles anymore." His eyes held Milly's for a moment. "I wish someone would just take them."

Three days later, Milly again found herself in the alley with her father. This time he was looking at an old iron grate. "You know, we used to take this up to the mountains in deer season all the time. It worked really good," *Corbett Lawyer explained.* "You could build a nice little fire under it for cooking, but I bet you could heat up all kinds of different things." *He turned to Milly with a smile.* "It's gettin' kinda rusty. I'm thinking of getting a new one. I don't need this one anymore." *Just like that, Milly could heat her sweathouse rocks.*

"Then one night I found this tin leaning against the bank of the canal." Milly pointed to the sweathouse roof and her voice grew serious. "Dad wants you to get better, too, May. Maybe our old ways will help." Corbett Lawyer was tired of seeing children die.

May's eyes glistened with gratitude for Milly's act of love. It was all the thanks Milly would ever need. Nonetheless, May asked, "What's the Nez Perce word for 'thanks'?"

"*Qe'ciyéw'yew'*[3]," Milly replied.

"*Qe'ciyéw'yew'*, my Sister." May looked into Milly's eyes and smiled.

They talked into the night, tossing drops of water on the rocks whenever the air cooled, until their shadows on the blanket-covered walls grew fainter and fainter. Their skin glistening from the sweathouse bath, Milly led May to a rock crevice spring that filled a small pool. The giggling girls took turns dousing each other with cooling water,

---

[3] kəts\ē\YAU\yau

dried themselves with towels Milly had ready, and Milly braided May's blue-black waist-long hair. They dressed and retraced their steps back to May's window. Several times, Milly waited as May stopped to catch her breath.

Milly helped May step through the raised window. Back inside the dormitory, May turned one final time, reached for Milly's hand and whispered the six words Milly would never forget. "I will always be with you."

Milly sadly walked home and tried to fill her heart with hope. It was all she could do.

But May did not get better. The day at Spalding Park, all afternoon in soaked boots, left May weakened from fever, and she never recovered. A few days after her sweat with Milly, she was moved to one of the beds in the ward for dying children. It was just a matter of time. May died before Milly could give her back her knife.

2

Cold mud stuck to Milly's father's and grandfather's shovels as they covered May's grave dug under the branches of a hackberry tree. Milly's mother and three elderly Presbyterian Indians were also in attendance for the short service. The chilly early April morning air was musty from the thawing earth.

Milly's grandfather, Archie Lawyer, spoke about life and death, the white man's heaven, and about

Indian beliefs. Reverend Lawyer was the last of the original Indian ministers, trained in the strict traditions of the Presbyterian Church. He prayed that May's spirit would be at peace here, so far away from home. The tiny group sang several hymns in Nez Perce. Milly attended many of these services. Sometimes it was only Milly, her mother and father, and her grandfather. She did not mind doing this. She felt she should be there when another child was buried.

They trod across the cheat grass, laid flat from the winter snow pack. Pockets of ice filled hoof prints of long-gone United States Army cavalry horses, pastured on this steep patch a half century ago.

If May had died in January, The Moon of Cold Wind That Shakes the Lodges, her small, simple wooden coffin could have been sent home by train, her body frozen by winter wind blowing through the slats of a railroad car. But May's soul must remain in Lapwai, many miles from home, among the forgotten unmarked graves of children.

3

In 1915, Milly graduated from Lapwai High School. Four years later, she earned a teaching certificate from Oregon State University and landed a position teaching Home Economics at an Indian girls' boarding school in Oregon. Milly poured her heart into her work. The school became well known for innovations. Unwed Indian teenage mothers were welcomed, their children cared for by dozens of young aunties.

Some girls were Warm Springs Indian, but none remembered May. Children sent away with tuberculosis seemed to disappear. Milly's memories dimmed, and May's knife remained forgotten in a dresser drawer in Lapwai.

In 1941, Milly's life changed again. Her mother became ill, and Milly returned home to care for her. Several years later, she became Auntie to the first of her sister Beatrice's three children. They visited often from nearby Lewiston. Gordy, the youngest, spent summers on the reservation.

4

1963

Gordy's grandmother needed constant rest. He escaped the imposed silence by wandering the hills just behind his aunt's house. The hills continued south behind the fort grounds, a mile from the village, and formed the western edge of narrow Lapwai Valley. Valley of the Butterflies. His accomplice on these adventures was his next door neighbor, a red-haired white boy named Sam, who Gordy's grandfather, Corbett Lawyer, nicknamed Redwing.

"You boys can have some pie and then go play upstairs," Aunt Milly called out one day.

"Okay, Auntie," Sam and Gordy replied together. It was raining, or they would have been working on their horse trap. It was another of Sam's big ideas his friends usually went along with. His lopsided grin seemed to seal the deal. They were digging a big hole along the bottom of the hill behind their houses where Harold Miller's horses ran back and forth. They planned to cover the hole with branches and leaves and catch one of the horses. To two nine-year-old boys, this seemed like a logical idea. Sam and Gordy spent a lot of time unsupervised.

They finished pieces of lemon meringue pie at the kitchen table and treaded lightly upstairs. As long as they were quiet, Aunt Milly didn't care what they got into. One time they used a thirty-four star American flag Gordy's great, great-grandfather, The Lawyer, received before the first treaty with the whites as a tent.

There were a lot of interesting things to play with upstairs, but mostly they played with little army men. Because they were at Gordy's place, Sam usually had to be the Nazis while Gordy got to be the Americans. They instinctively avoided playing Cowboys and Indians.

Today, however, the boys were looking for something new. Underneath a flowered shawl and an old pair of moccasins in a dresser drawer, Sam found a small knife. On its bone casing a small nameplate read "Barlow."

"Gordy, look." Together they opened one of the blades and tested it on an old postcard found in the same drawer. The still-sharp blade slashed the paper in half.

"You want it?" asked Gordy. Sam's birthday was in September, and Gordy would be back in school in Lewiston. Sam always got Gordy a present on his birthday in June. Gordy wanted to give Sam something.

"Sure," Sam answered. May's knife had a new home.

5

Death tolls from tuberculosis steadily declined during the late 1930's, and the hospital in Lapwai closed in 1945. The school district acquired the sanatorium campus. The brick building at the base of the valley's western hills held the fourth, fifth, and sixth grades.

Everyone at Lapwai Elementary School knew the somber history of the school buildings. The elementary teachers were all locals, and the younger ones had themselves attended school there. There were stories of pencils stolen and assignments disappearing, but in an elementary school it's easy to blame ghosts for unfinished work.

The Indian teachers didn't like to talk about ghosts. Sometimes, though, the younger white teachers shared feelings that some nights, working late, they weren't alone.

Especially in Room Five in the Upper Building. Room Five had been the intensive care ward of the sanatorium. Children who died, died there. Room Five became a fourth grade classroom taught by Mrs. Preston. Sam was in Mrs. Preston's class.

Younger teachers were careful not to mention ghosts around Mrs. Preston. Her father had been a doctor at the sanatorium. She grew up nearby in the first floor apartment of a large house that decades earlier housed officers assigned to Fort Lapwai. Mrs. Preston was troubled by vivid memories of tiny bodies lying still in hospital beds in the very room where she now taught. When her husband was killed in an accident at the lumber mill in Lewiston, she moved back in with her frail 85-year-old mother. Mrs. Preston bore a weight of tragic sadness.

Sam's friend Denny lived in the second-floor apartment above Mrs. Preston. Like at Aunt Milly's house, Sam had to play quietly with his friend so Mrs. Preston's mother could rest.

Denny had two sisters. They played board games together and told stories. Cindy, the oldest at 13, told of odd things she saw and heard in the hills and in the canal behind their house. She was a serious girl, not the kind to make things up, so the younger children believed her.

Cindy enjoyed taking a blanket and a book to a thicket of hackberry trees behind the old cavalry stables to spend warm spring afternoons reading. It was an interesting place. The ground was oddly rounded in shapes about her size. One day she came home to tell Denny, their younger sister Vicky, and Sam that she heard voices speaking unfamiliar Indian languages, yet no one was in sight. Cindy recognized Nez Perce. She often helped her mother at the post office, where elderly Nez Perce women, dressed in long flowered dresses and beaded moccasins, met to visit in their native tongue. Children in Lapwai, both Indian and white, knew many common Nez Perce words.

Cindy also said that several times at night she saw the outline of an Indian girl her age walking the canal behind their house. The canal cut a deep channel at the base of the hill. Denny could see it from his bedroom window. When Sam stayed all night at Denny's, they watched for the shape Cindy described.

6

"Sam, do you have something to show everyone?" asked Mrs. Preston after the class sang "Happy Birthday" to him. He forgot about bringing a birthday show-and-tell. He felt in his pocket.

"This is from my friend who lives in Lewiston," Sam said as he held up the shiny pocket knife.

"Wow!" his classmates exclaimed.

Sam took good care of his knife. His father and he sharpened their knives with whetstones together on the front porch after Mr. Evans got home from work.

Throughout the rest of the morning Sam's classmates pestered him to let them hold the beautiful knife. Finally, Mrs. Preston said, "Since we can't seem to get our work done, I'm going to keep Sam's knife on my desk. Sam, you can get it after school." Sam brought his knife to the front of the classroom and laid it next to a small hand bell on Mrs. Preston's big oak desk.

As Sam was getting his lunch box from the cloak room at the end of the day, his friend Luke walked over.

"You wanna come over and see our new dog?"

"Yeah! What's his name?"

"Aussie."

Sam forgot all about picking up his knife from Mrs. Preston's desk.

Sam and Luke played until dinnertime, when Sam discovered he had forgotten his knife. It was too late to walk back to school. It would have to wait until the next day.

Sam woke early the next morning, bolted a bowl of cereal, and ran most of the way to school. He was the first student there. Mrs. Preston stood behind her desk, staring straight ahead, as if at something long unseen. Her eyes were filled with haunted sorrow. Sam walked to the empty place on her desk where he had left the knife and asked Mrs. Preston if she knew where it was.

"I'm sorry, Sam. I saw it here after school. I had to go to a meeting, but I thought you might come right back, so I left it here. I asked Eldon if he saw anyone come in, but he said nobody was around by then except teachers."

Sam didn't know what to say. He knew in his heart that the kind old janitor wouldn't steal from anyone. "Can I look for it?" he asked.

"I'll help you," answered Mrs. Preston. But she knew they wouldn't find it. In a low voice she said to herself, "One of *them* took it."

PART ONE
State

The 1971-1972 Lapwai (Idaho) High School
Basketball Team

Back Row (Left to Right): Coach Ray McNeese; Paul Weston (JV/Varsity); Larry "Junior" Sams; Denny Smith; Sam Evans; Mike McNeese; Tim Weber (JV/Varsity); Jesse Waters

Front Row (Left to Right): Manager Steve Holt; Luke Woods; Billy White; Terry Gibson; Robert "Sonny" Reuben; Jimmy Redjacket; Manager Ken Hodges

1

1971

At the end of the third quarter of the junior varsity game, the varsity players rise. They sit together, or with girlfriends holding hands. Walking from the deep, wooden balcony seats of the Wildcat's Lair student section, down the hallway stairs to the locker room, they hear their town's applause. The pep band plays, "Cheer, cheer for old Lapwai High..."

Sam dreamed of this moment since he was eight, running up and down the polished marble hallways with his friends as their older brothers warmed up. He is so proud it's almost impossible to keep his Warrior Look on his face and not bust out smiling as he makes his way to the dingy grey locker room.

The boys are dressed in matching blazers, young men in clip-on ties. Two of the Indian boys wear beaded medallions over white turtlenecks.

The Wildcats' new coach, Ray McNeese, wasn't too happy about that. He told them, "Wear a white shirt and tie." Discipline doesn't leave room for interpretation, he believed, or real soon things break down. "It's going to be a little trickier coaching here," Coach McNeese realized. "They want to do things their way, but they know their basketball. Too much run-and-gun, but they feel it." The boys came to the first practice with more basketball savvy than he'd ever seen: straight up on jump shots, dribble with either hand, looking for 'backdoor' cuts...the Indian boys and the white boys. "They'll have to learn how to play defense," Coach McNeese thought to himself, "but we could give some people trouble at State."

Sam had a good sophomore year, starting on the junior varsity, averaging nine rebounds a game. Last year on varsity he came off the bench when one of the starters got in foul trouble.

But Coach McNeese brought his own 'big man.' His son Mike, at six foot five, was two inches taller than Sam and started the previous two years at Craigmont. Sam believed in signs. He thought of the upcoming basketball season and concluded, "Oh, well. I guess that's just the way it is."

Sam and Mike got to know each other in the fall. Sam's father was the math teacher for the juniors and seniors and coached the football team. He remembered his difficult first year at Lapwai 14 years earlier, so Sam's parents invited the McNeeses over almost every weekend. Mike was pretty cool, thought Sam.

"How's it going?" Sam asked Mike one warm September Sunday afternoon. They were shooting baskets at the outdoor courts at the elementary school.

"I don't know. Some kids are calling me names."

"Like what?"

"Like Stretch or Tower or Timber," mumbled Mike.

Mike didn't know the other boys at Lapwai High School yet. He sat alone in class. He didn't play football, so he spent most afternoons shooting by himself in the empty high school gymnasium. He didn't know the names the boys went by. Swiggs. Bones. Skinner. Wa-doo. Stungy...

"The Indians are just naming you, man. That's good."

"Like your name, Counts, the back-up center for the Lakers?"

"Yeah, Mel Counts. Tall white guy."

"What should I do?"

"Just get rebounds, enit?" Sam answered.

Lapwai Wildcats Versus Culdesac Wolves

Pre-season practices went well for Mike. Coach McNeese liked to work the ball inside, but Mike deftly passed back out to open players. He set solid screens at the top of the key for Sonny Reuben or Billy White driving to the basket. His aggressive rebounding and unselfish attitude garnered his teammates' respect. Mike began to get their humor.

To his surprise, he was starting to have fun at Lapwai.

For the season's first away game, the Wildcats traveled eight miles south to Culdesac. They would play three Class A-4 teams before starting league competition. The smaller White Pine League teams could be tough. Last year, Culdesac and Lapwai were tied at halftime before the Wildcats pulled away.

Not so this year. None of the Wolves could stop Mike. When they went to a sagging zone, Jesse Waters and Denny got hot from outside. The Wildcats led 20-0 at the end of the first quarter. Coach McNeese shook his head. He'd never held a team scoreless for a quarter before. Sam, Luke, and the rest of the second string played the entire second half.

Lapwai Wildcats Versus Troy Trojans

The Wildcats next beat Troy 59-40. Even though the boys wanted to fast-break, Coach McNeese slowed it down to work on their half-court offense. The second string started the fourth quarter. Everyone was getting playing time.

Their third game of the season was similar. Elk River was also just plain out-manned, and Coach McNeese used the opportunity to try different presses and zones.

Lapwai Wildcats Versus Latah Valley Falcons

The league opener promised to be a very different story. Latah Valley was the defending A-4 state champions, and since Latah Valley High School's enrollment surpassed 120 students the previous year, they moved up to the A-3 classification. Three starters returned for the Falcons. Ron Harper made All-State as a junior and already signed a letter-of-intent to play at the University of Idaho.

As the Wildcats entered the gymnasium an hour before the JV game, Latah Valley's side was already nearly full. Their uniforms and warm-up jackets slung over their shoulders, the boys were greeted by a sound familiar to Lapwai people: the hand-over-the-mouth 'Indian war whoop' from old westerns.

Mike was stunned. He had never been on this side of a cultural line before. He felt a sudden flash of embarrassment and anger. Tension charged the air between him and Sonny walking beside him. He didn't know what to say or do, but Sonny remained stolid in the face of this insulting gesture. The sound faded as they entered the visiting team's locker room to hang up their uniforms, but the message was clear. This game wasn't just against five other boys.

6:00 PM

The JV's were rattled. They were usually a solid group of younger talent. When they scrimmaged the varsity, they made the older boys work. Tonight they turned the ball over time after time. They sulked off the court with a 21 point loss.

8:00 PM

Many Friday nights on the road Lapwai fans outnumbered the home side. A long line of car lights would snake along the Clearwater River or up and down the rolling hills of the Camas Prairie. But on a Tuesday night, the only Wildcat supporters were a handful of family members.

The Latah Valley crowd jeered every Wildcat mistake. Meanwhile, Ron Harper was having a very good first half. At six foot two, he could penetrate the middle of the key or hit pull-up jumpers.

At halftime Ron had 18 points, but the Wildcats trailed by only nine, due to Coach McNeese's disciplined, ball control approach. If the fast break wasn't there, they brought it back out front and ran the offense. Denny hit three shots in a row from the corner, and Sonny found Mike open underneath several times. The Wildcats were still very much in the game.

Coach McNeese was normally a yeller. He had plenty to yell about tonight. He harped on taking care of the basketball, and the team already had 12 turnovers. He could start there.

Something stopped him. He could only guess how the boys felt about the anger directed at them. But something was happening inside the silent locker room. The stunned look was gone. In his players' eyes pride began to take over.

The boys had known bigotry all their lives. Walking down Main Street in Lewiston together in their navy blue letterman's jackets, they heard the comments whispered from behind. When they walked into stores, they felt the eyes following them. Shared experiences made these boys more than just teammates.

Billy was assigned to guard Ron Harper. He stood by himself, clenching and unclenching his fists. When Mr. McNeese called the team together, he sat at the end of the bench staring ahead.

Coach McNeese talked about all five hustling back on defense. He said that if they set high post screens, Jesse, with his quickness, could drive the lane and draw some fouls on Harper. This is what the Wildcats needed to hear: they needed someone to believe in them. The nerves were gone. They were ready to go back out and play ball.

As the Wildcats ran back onto the court, their families' cheers drowned out a few scattered boos. The Falcons emerged from their locker room to a thunderous roar, but a different Wildcat team lined up against them for the second half tip-off.

8:45 PM

Billy stepped in front of the first pass to Ron Harper and found Denny for an easy lay-in. Seven points down.

Billy stayed on Ron like a glove. When Harper started throwing elbows, Billy smiled. This was like his first summer on the Pine Ridge Reservation in

Sioux Country when he stayed with his mother's family. "Teach the Nez Perce kid a lesson," he heard from the other boys.

"Piece of cake," thought Billy. He was starting to have fun.

The Falcons grew frustrated. When Latah Valley set double screens for Harper and the Wildcats switched, he was still shadowed step-for-step.

The crowd turned ugly and yelled at their own players. When a large woman stood and shouted, "Someone stop that Indian!" as Sonny drove the length of the court, the referee slapped Latah Valley with a technical. Sonny sank both free throws, and the Falcons led by one with a minute-and-a-half left.

With the technical, the Wildcats kept possession. They took a full minute off the clock moving the ball around the perimeter. A Falcon grabbed Jesse to force free throws. Jesse made both shots. Wildcats by one. Ron brought the ball up himself and forced up an awkward shot that somehow found its way through the hoop. With 23 seconds left, the Falcons pressed. Coach McNeese yelled to Sonny to call time-out, and they went over breaking Latah Valley's trap.

Jesse got the ball, and Sonny set a screen for Billy, who streaked down court. Jesse faked to Sonny, but hit Billy with a long 'baseball' pass. Mike stood wide open underneath the basket, and Billy quickly flung an overhead pass to him. But instead of making the easy shot and giving the ball back to Latah Valley with enough time to score, Mike kicked it out to Denny on the wing. As three Falcons converged on him, Denny passed back to Mike with three seconds on the clock. Mike dropped it in. Game over.

The Wildcats huddled for the customary "One, two, three...Latah Valley" cheer and shook hands with a sullen Falcon team. The subdued hometown crowd filed down the bleachers and out the gym doors to their cars and pickups.

The Wildcats waited until the locker room to celebrate. Jesse shouted to Billy, "I didn't think us Indi'ns played defense!"

"Must've been my Sioux half, enit?" Billy laughed.

Coach McNeese shook hands with each player, telling the starters, "Heckuva second half," and saying to Sam and the other reserves, "Next time."

Coach McNeese and JV coach Earl Guerreros decided it might not be the best idea for the whole team to all go into Latah Valley's one restaurant for something to eat. While they waited on the bus, Coach McNeese ordered hamburgers to-go for the hungry teenage boys.

They headed home. After tossing his paper sack in the cardboard box Coach McNeese carried up and down the bus aisle, Sam leaned forward and rested his head against the seat in front of him. Next to him an exhausted Billy laid his head on Sam's back and fell asleep.

2

That Saturday the Wildcats handled Timberline 63 to 48. At the final buzzer, Jessica Whitehawk dashed down the long, dark school hallway to the band room and quickly disassembled her clarinet. She snapped the case shut and hurried out the band room door. Her family was waiting.

"Grandpa needs the horn," she understood. "But I wish I could watch him play tonight." The Nezpercians had a gig that evening at the Pi-Nee-Waus Community Center. It was Josiah Whitehawk who started her playing the clarinet. He'd been in the all-Indian jazz orchestra from the beginning, in 1929. The members were getting older, and there were fewer of them, but they still loved performing the old-school dance numbers.

Just then, Jessica's two younger sisters came sprinting around the corner and flung themselves onto her slender legs. Despite her disappointment, she smiled as she looked at their carefree faces.

"I'm their *nén*[4]. It's my job to take care of my little sisters," she knew. They hurried outside. Ida

Whitehawk had the car already warm and running. She rolled down the window and greeted her daughter.

"Hey, girl...thanks, *'áyat*[5], for watching the kids. Grandpa really wants us to hear 'em play tonight. He doesn't know how many more of these he's got left in him."

"It's good, Mom," Jessica replied. "Are we goin' up to Cousins'?" Ida Whitehawk nodded.

"There's some pot pies you can warm up for dinner after these two burn off some energy." Jessica's sisters bounced on her feet and pulled on her arms. "We'll pick you up after the dance."

They jumped in the big family station wagon and drove to the part of town known as the Agency. It was once the site of the U.S. Army's Fort Lapwai and later the tuberculosis hospital and boarding school for Indian children. Lapwai School District now owned the property. There was plenty of room for kids to run and play on the playground equipment installed outside Room Five.

The three sisters tramped tracks in the snow for Fox and Goose, made snow angels, and swung high in the air to bail out into deep piles of snow. The silhouette Jessica cast in the moonlight seemed only slightly larger than her little sisters'. Her long hair swirled wildly as she chased them, and her

---

[4] nān

[5] Ī\it

footsteps were as light as a deer's. Gradually the little ones tired.

That's when Jessica felt it. The eyes. It happened every time they played there. She slid off her swing and searched the bushes beside the playground. Her back to the tall windows of Room Five, she felt the eyes pore deep inside her. She slowly turned. Staring into the shadows formed by the globe stand and the coat rack near Mrs. Preston's desk, she crept forward.

Jessica's sisters stopped swinging and approached their big sister. They each took a hand and gently tugged. Jessica stopped, looked toward their worried faces, and smiled. She mustn't scare them. It was one of the many ways she was supposed to protect her sisters.

"Are you ready for some hot chocolate?" Jessica offered. They nodded excitedly and gathered mittens and gloves tossed aside earlier. Jessica looked back once at Room Five and then led her sisters to the warmth and safety of their aunt's nearby home.

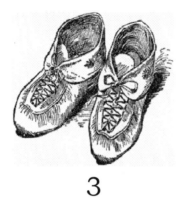

3

Mike was thinking about asking Sonny's younger sister Julia to the Winter Dance. Julia was a varsity cheerleader, and Mike usually found a way to sit near her during the JV games on road trips.

"Do you think Julia would go with me to the Winter Dance?" Mike asked Sam in Senior English class.

"Yeah. Denny took her to Homecoming."

"It's okay with her family and everything?"

"Sure. You play basketball, so you're okay with them. Sonny's mom goes to all the games."

"What should I do?"

"Just do the regular stuff. You should ask her this week, though. Get a corsage from Lewiston. Maybe you and Sonny could double-date. He'll probably go with Vicky. She and Julia are like sisters."

In matching blue and white pleated skirts and vee-neck cheerleader sweaters, with the same slight figure, delicate features, and straight hair that flipped up at the shoulder, Julia was just a calmer version of Vicky. Except for one tiny difference, the girls could have been mistaken for twins.

"You think Julia likes to dance?" Mike asked.

"Oh, she's a really good dancer. You should see her at pow-wows. She usually wins prize money. There's a big pow-wow here in February."

"Can we go to pow-wows?"

Sam looked at Mike strangely. Sam had to remember that Lapwai was the only world he'd ever known. This life was all new to Mike.

"Yeah, white people go. We'll all go and watch Jimmy hoop dance. It's really cool." Jimmy Redjacket was the second-string point guard. A junior, he would probably start next year. "Maybe Julia will ask you to round dance with her, enit?" Sam teased.

Mike had more questions about pow-wows, but he wanted to ask about Julia.

"What kind of music does she like?"

"She's like Sonny: soul music, big time."

"What else should we talk about?"

"Gawd, Mike, she's a regular girl. Talk about movies. Talk about basketball, I don't know."

"Is there anything I shouldn't talk about?"

Sam turned very still. After a long pause he replied, "Don't talk about ghosts."

4

"Last year we were coming back from playing Grangeville, and Billy started talking about weird stuff he seen when he was huntin' outside of Grangeville up around Dixie. Weird noises in the trees and stuff like that. Then..."

"Did you guys win?" Mike interrupted.

"Yeah. Did you guys?"

"No, we got beat."

"Yeah, well, Jesse and me and Luke were telling about how last year before football we ran down to Spalding to break in our new cleats, and we took the back road over Thunder Hill. Right by the little graveyard there was this shadow on the ground, but no trees around. We called it Long Shad..."

"That's why you guys always say, 'Long Shadow'!" Mike interrupted again.

"Yeah. When you see or hear something weird say, 'Long Shadow'."

"Anyway," Sam continued, "everybody's thinking of stories about weird things, and then Sonny starts talking. Everybody got real quiet to listen to Sonny, 'cause you know how Sonny hardly ever talks? He was tellin' about how he gets woken up in the middle of the night by his bed shaking. His house is one of the new ones across from the creek."

"Yeah, I dropped him off after practice last night."

"So Sonny says he thinks they built those new houses without telling anyone they found graves, 'cause then they couldn't build there. He thinks his house is over a grave. He said sometimes it feels like somebody else is in the room."

Sam continued. "Sonny said that Julia has the same thing happen to her, and she gets really scared. She doesn't want to talk about it. Other Indians wouldn't either."

"Why don't they talk about ghosts?" Mike asked.

"Just the way it is. Nez Perce believe the spiritual world is all around us. It's called the Dreamer religion, or Seven Drums. If you see a car go by with a drum tied on top, they're probably going to an old-style Indian funeral. You should, like, not laugh around 'til they go by." Mike nodded.

Sam went on. "Some Indians have guardian spirits who give special powers, but if you don't follow the traditions, the power can act against you."

"So do, like, Sonny and Jesse have guardian spirits?"

"I don't know," Sam shrugged. "They wouldn't say anyway, because the power would be diminished. They can only talk about it with elders who help them understand their guardian spirits."

"They have to prepare to receive their guardian spirits," Sam continued. "It's all really traditional. You know, we all hang out together, playing hoops and everything, but when Sonny and them go off to the mountains, I don't know what they do. Jesse, he spends all summer in Oregon. So I don't know about their guardian spirits."

"How do you know all this?" Mike wondered.

"Just lucky, I guess. Just hanging around my old neighbors, Aunt Milly's place," Sam explained.

"My friend Gordy stayed there a lot, and we had to be real quiet in the house, so sometimes Aunt Milly told us stories. Then she started teaching Gordy traditional ways, and I was just there. It was cool." Sam paused.

"She was passing Indian beliefs down. I think Aunt Milly's like a medicine woman or something." A silence fell.

Mike returned to the bus ride from Grangeville. "What else did Sonny say?"

"That's all he said, but it was really freaky. Everybody stopped talking 'til we were like by Winchester, and then some people started talking about other stuff."

"Are there really graveyards around?" asked Mike.

"Yeah, but they're pretty hard to find. There's this one just up the road from my house on the hill where you turn to go up Soldiers Grade. I used to go up there with my friend Gordy I was telling you about when I was a kid. Some of the grave markers are written in Nez Perce. It's really cool."

"I heard there's this one for Indian kids from other tribes who died at a hospital that's the elementary school now," Sam added. "You know, where we play basketball all the time. I wonder where that graveyard is. I'd like to find it."

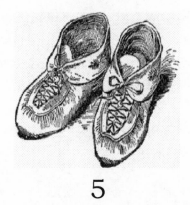

5

Sam stood with Luke and Jimmy in a long line waiting for their Christmas cookies the Home Economics classes made for everyone. It was the last day before Christmas vacation! They had a short assembly at the end of the day. The junior high and high school bands played songs from the winter concert. Next, the chorus sang three funny songs about Christmas. Then everyone sang Christmas carols. Finally, Reverend Matthews, the Indian counselor, led the students in singing "When the Roll Is Called Up Yonder" in Nez Perce. "Wewanekitpa himuna, wewanekitpa himunu..." The students loved singing that song together. Even the white farm kids who didn't hang out with Indian kids much knew the words.

After he got his cookies, Sam went to the gym, took his shoes off, and shot around until all the teachers and students were gone; he planned to sneak onto the gym stage and cut pieces off the huge paper roll kept there for sledding that night.

The school principal, Carl Richardson, knew what Sam was up to. He had done the same thing himself when he grew up in Lapwai 19 years earlier. Besides school events, there were few activities or places to go for restless teenagers. Most of the things they did involved small illegalities: trespassing, curfew breaking, or other minor infractions that 'weren't going to hurt anyone.'

The pulp mill in Lewiston donated a 40-inch-wide roll of heavyweight paper every year to the school. The student council used the paper to cover the gym floor for the annual Fall Fun Carnival. The paper was even waxed on one side, perfect for sledding. There was practically no way to control its direction. So much the better.

Maybe the mill owners wanted to do something nice for Lapwai for the 'fragrance' that sometimes drifted the twelve miles from Lewiston to Lapwai. In Nez Perce County they call the odor The Smell of Money. In addition, many mill workers were from Lapwai, both Indian and white. The mill could afford small donations every now and then to the Lapwai community.

Everyone was going to meet up at dark. Fresh snow fell all day, as if by magic, preparing the hill for the night's festivities.

The steep hill behind the old Army cavalry stables made for excellent sledding. No one ever paid attention to what kids did there. They kept a '48 Cadillac car hood leaned against the stables. A couple of times up and down the hill with that massive snow packer, and the kids had an excellent run.

Toward the bottom, near a grove of hackberry trees, the hill took on a strange contour. The slope rolled in a series of mounds running horizontally to the hillside. The mounds seemed almost man-made. With each bump sledders picked up speed. The path ended at a neglected gravel road.

As expected, nearly all the older high school students who lived in town were there. Junior Sams brought a half-dozen old tires, and a nice fire was blazing. Sam brought enough paper sleds for everyone. Some kids rode together, flailing their arms to stay in the snow trough. After a few runs, Mike and Julia ended up at the top of the hill at the same time, and Mike boldly asked Julia if she wanted to slide down together. Julia didn't seem to mind the idea. They careened out of control, using their arms more to grab each other than to guide themselves down the wicked hill. They crashed through the snow where the run banked away from the hackberry trees and came to a stop a few feet from the side of the stables.

Sam was following closely behind. He soared off the track through the hole in the snow wall, but instead of plowing on top of the human pile that was Mike and Julia, he managed to dig his right arm into the deep snow and veer to the side.

Sam came to a halt under the largest of the hackberry trees. A big grin covered his face: crashing was the best part. As he rolled toward the tree to get up, his eye caught a metallic glint reflecting the tire-fire's flames. When he looked more closely, Sam's expression suddenly changed. A small knife was placed on a smooth rock against the tree trunk. Branches were woven together above the knife, sheltering it from snow. On its bone casing was a tiny nameplate, with a single word written in the center: *Barlow*.

6

"What happened? You look like you saw a ghost," Mike asked as Julia, Sam, and he brushed off snow and started back up the hill. He glimpsed at Julia, hoping she didn't hear what he just said.

"It's really weird…"

"Long Shadow?"

"Yeah, definitely Long Shadow. Lootz!" Sam shouted to Luke walking ahead of them. "Remember in fourth grade I had this knife that just disappeared in Mrs. Preston's room?"

Luke stopped to think. "Barely. Tell me more."

"You just got Aussie. I went over to your house, and I forgot to get my knife back from Mrs. Pres…"

"Oh, yeah! Wasn't it a pretty nice knife? I remember it was really shiny and had something written on it, and it was kinda like…"

"Kinda like this?" And Sam held up the knife for Luke to see in the firelight.

7

The varsity players watched the tall, skinny red-haired sophomore take off from the middle of the key and slam a small, kids' basketball home. They were impressed.

That was Sam two years ago. Two inches taller now, he was probably the best jumper on the team, but he just couldn't rebound against the better teams. He reached over shorter players and got called for fouls. He would get a hand on the ball, but not bring it down. Sometimes he just slapped it to a teammate. Christmas vacation, that all changed.

Before practice, Mike taught Sam to move his feet, watch the flight of the ball, turn his body to the basket, and block-out with his hips.

Coach McNeese noticed Sam's improvement. One day, he left the towels he was folding on the training table and showed Sam how to put his hands back to find exactly where his man was positioned.

Tip-ins came easily. Sam had excellent timing. When the ball came off the rim, he was a good eight inches above it for a soft tap.

For a break, Coach McNeese arranged a scrimmage with his former team from Craigmont. They were good ballplayers. Three years earlier they finished fourth at State. Mrs. McNeese ran the scoreboard.

Now the Craigmont boys were either going to college or working on local farms. They weren't in the best of shape, but they could still play.

The two sides traded baskets for a few minutes, when Coach McNeese surprised everyone by putting Sam in for Denny. He was assigned to guard a big old boy named Doug Barton. Sam remembered watching Doug Barton in eighth grade. He was The Man. He led the Huskies in both rebounds and points. He was very good.

After Doug graduated he played at Treasure Valley Community College in Oregon one year, but missed home, so he joined the family business. Doug still had basketball skills, but sitting behind the wheel of a grain truck 12 hours a day did not prepare him for this. After two or three times up and down the court, Doug's hands were on his knees as he tried to catch his breath.

Sam was thrilled to be on the court with the first string. He worked hard getting position on Doug. When Sam tipped in one of Sonny's jumpers, Denny went crazy on the bench.

A few minutes later, Coach McNeese put Denny back in. He met Sam on the court and slapped him on the shoulder. "That's it, Sam. That's what I'm looking for." Later, Sam gave Jesse a breather, and in the second half, played underneath for Mike.

Coach McNeese felt very good about the day. He enjoyed seeing his old players again, but most of all he thought, "Now we got a solid big man to come in off the bench." The pieces were falling in place for the 'Cats' second half of the season.

8

"Haven't seen you out here for a while, Sammy," Mr. Evans said as Sam joined him on the front porch with his knife and his whetstone.

"Haven't had a good knife for a while."

"Is that the knife you lost a couple of years ago?"

"Yeah, it..."

"Say, 'Yes,' Sammy."

"Okay...yes... It was eight years ago."

"Where'd you find it?"

"We were sledding behind the horse barn, and I rolled off and it was right there under a tree laying on a rock."

"Long Shadow!" Coach Evans grinned.

Sam looked at his father, surprised, and smiled. Lapwai High School students had their own language- English, random Nez Perce words, favorite words from Spanish class, Indian speaking mannerisms, made-up words, and odd phrases they invented. Hearing their students' chatter all day, the high school teachers spoke fluent Lapwai.

"Where were you all sledding again?" asked Coach Evans.

"Behind the old Army horse barn."

"Did you ask anyone if you could go there?"

"We didn't think it was anyone's land, like maybe just the tribe's or something."

"Well, every place is somebody's land."

"Do you know whose land that is, Dad?"

"I do happen to know. It's Josiah Whitehawk's."

"That elder Mom always sits with at the basketball games? He's cool. I like his hat," Sam responded. Josiah Whitehawk wore a classic ten-gallon hat with a beaded band.

"Have you ever noticed what Mr. Whitehawk does with popcorn at the basketball games?" Sam shook his head. "He pours it into his hat and then shares it with your mom."

"That's cool."

"He's a really nice man. He would really appreciate it if you and one of the Indian boys would visit him. I'm sure he'll say it's okay to use his land. It would just be the respectful thing to do. That's all he wants. But I know you know that. He probably would like to talk basketball. I don't think he's missed a home game in 20 years."

"How do you know so much about him?"

"Well, after they started visiting at games, your mom told me that Mr. Whitehawk was upset about how much money he got after wheat harvest from land he leased to Pete Bailey. So I went to his place and explained that the price of wheat was way down. Because he and your mom are friends, he trusts me. We started talking about his allotment land that..."

"What's that, Dad?" Sam interrupted.

"Allotment land is what each Indian family got after the last treaty. But a lot of families sold their land to settlers at bad prices, so the government passed a law that Indians could rent their land to whites, but not sell it. Mr. Whitehawk has all the land behind the cavalry stables. A lot of it's too steep to farm, though."

"Should I just go to his house?"

"You know his granddaughter Jessica? She's a sophomore. You could ask her to talk to her grandfather first."

Sam knew Jessica Whitehawk from band. She played clarinet. He could talk to her when they got back to school about a time to visit her grandfather.

"I know you boys will do the right thing, Sammy."

"Thanks. We always clean up after we have a fire, and we always close the gate."

"That's good."

"Thanks, Dad. This was interesting. I always wondered why there were only a couple of Indian farmers." Sam paused. "I'm glad I found my knife."

"It seems like it found you," Coach Evans finished with a smile.

9

Sam didn't have to wait until school started again to talk to Jessica Whitehawk. The boys went to the Pi-Nee-Waus, "The Buildin'," for some pick-up games with players from the Nez Perce Nation team, young men who were on the Lapwai High School varsity when Sam was in junior high. They had just gotten back from winning an all-Indian tournament in Wapato, Washington. It was a good workout and a lot of fun. Defense was not emphasized.

Jessica was with two other sophomore girls sharing a large order of French fries at the Pi-Nee-Waus Café. Sam waited until Jessica was alone, looking at songs on the jukebox, before talking to her about visiting her grandfather.

This was the first time Sam had ever talked to Jessica Whitehawk alone. "She's really pretty," Sam realized. "Her long hair looks cool." Jessica shyly listened as Sam explained the purpose of his visit.

"Grandpa is coming into town today. I'll talk to him. I can tell you what he says tomorrow at this same time." Sam looked forward to talking to Jessica again. He joined the other boys in the gym, they played another half-court game to 50, and Sam walked home.

The following day Sam waited for Jessica in the Pi-Nee-Waus hallway. He told the boys he would join them soon in the gym. Today he didn't want to be sweaty and stinky when he talked to Jessica.

"Grandpa says to come up tomorrow around ten, ten-thirty...you know, Indian Time," Jessica informed him.

"Thanks," Sam replied. He paused a moment and decided to go for it. "Do you want to go sledding tomorrow? A bunch of people are going. I could give you a ride." Jessica lived two miles north of town by Thunder Hill.

"I'll ask my mom. Is there drinking? She won't let me go if people are drinking."

"No, we're being good. We don't want to get caught and mess up going to State."

"Okay. She'll probably let me go. You can just come by."

"It'll be about five."

"That sounds good."

"Okay. I'll see ya. Qe'ciyéw'yew'."

"*Eehé[6],*" Jessica turned with a smile. "You're welcome." She was glad the tall white boy knew some Nez Perce.

As Sam walked past the gym door to the locker room with a big smile on his face, Luke shouted, "Counts! What's with you? You look like you just scored, enit? Háamt'ic! We're waiting for you."

---

[6] a\HE

10

Sam and Jesse drove Sam's old green Studebaker pickup to Josiah Whitehawk's house. They put some sand bags in the back for extra weight driving in the snow. Josiah Whitehawk lived about six miles outside of town up a rarely plowed gravel road.

Mr. Whitehawk's one-room cabin lay snugly against the hillside of a small draw off Garden Gulch Road. Smoke rose from a handmade barrel woodstove, and a well-worn path led from the front door to a large woodpile of short pieces of two-by-fours and stove length logs of locust, hackberry, and cottonwood.

When Sam and Jesse tapped on the old wooden door, they could see Mr. Whitehawk through the window shuffling toward the door, his head bent downward. His hat sat on a side table next to an overstuffed sofa covered with an old Pendleton blanket.

As Mr. Whitehawk opened the door and recognized his visitors, he straightened and broke out in a wide smile. "It's about time you two came so I could teach you how to play basketball, enit? Like in the old days, when we used to beat everybody. Come in. It's cold out here."

"Qe'ciyéw'yew', Uncle," Jesse responded. They made their way to the sofa, carefully stepping over a sleeping dog.

"Never mind him. He's older than I am," Josiah Whitehawk chortled.

After everyone was seated, Sam started. "Mr. Whitehawk, we came to...," but Jesse elbowed him.

"Not yet," Jesse whispered.

"We want to thank you on behalf of all the basketball team for being our Number One Fan," Jesse said. Sam nodded in agreement. Elders have all day to visit, he remembered. They needed to slow down and gab first before getting to the point. Indian time.

Mr. Whitehawk smiled. "So, how can I help you? The team looks pretty good this year. That new *sooyáapoo*[7] is pretty good for a white boy, enit, Sammy?" Sam smiled at Josiah Whitehawk's teasing. "He should pass quicker sometimes to you and Sonny, Jesse, when you guys are open, though. That new coach, his dad, should let you loose, let you run. Indians can run all day, like antelope, enit?" Josiah Whitehawk chuckled. "You, Sammy, you can work on boxing out better, you'll get more rebounds and get to play more." Mr. Whitehawk

---

[7] sü\ē\YAP\ō

was getting excited now that he finally had someone to talk basketball with. His body rocked slightly, and his hands fiddled with the frayed edge of a flowered shawl covering the soft, well-worn chair where he sat.

"Yes, Uncle. That's good advice. I've been working on it."

"Good. And you, Jesse, you shoot pretty good, but you sometimes do what your dad used to do. He used to let his right arm stick out to the side when he shot, and then the ball goes off to the left." Jesse and Sam looked at each other, impressed. Josiah Whitehawk knew his basketball.

"Thanks, Uncle," Sam and Jesse said together.

"Okay. Good. Glad to help. We can't let those Kamiah Indians beat us." Mr. Whitehawk caught his breath. "Now...Jessica said you wanted to ask me something."

"Yes, Uncle," Sam started again. "We wanted to ask you if we could use your hill behind the old Army horse barn for sledding. It's a good spot."

"It's a really good spot," Mr. Whitehawk agreed. "Kids been goin' there for a long time. Sometimes they take old tires up to the top and have a fire..." He looked at Jesse and Sam with a twinkle in his eyes.

"We'll clean up if we have a fire, Uncle," Jesse promised.

"Good. I like to keep the land looking good. It's been in my family a long time. I just want you to do one thing."

"What's that, Uncle?" Jesse asked.

"Just stay away from the graves."

11

"Graves?!" Jesse and Sam exclaimed together.

"Yes. There are quite a few of them. My father donated the land for a place for the little ones who passed away at the TB hospital. The ones from other tribes- the Spokanes, the Warm Springs, the Kootenais and them. The land was too steep to farm anyway, and it was close to the hospital. My father had a cousin who was there and got better, so he wanted to do something in return."

"Where are the graves, Uncle?" Sam asked.

"They're by some hackberry trees, just up from the barn. There aren't any markers or anything, but when you look at the ground, you can tell where they are." Jesse and Sam knew exactly where the graves were.

The room felt very quiet and somber. Josiah Whitehawk gazed sadly out the window. "A lot of my people are gone. They're buried all over the place. I hope... Anyway, you don't ever walk over graves, boys." Sam and Jesse nodded.

After a long pause, Mr. Whitehawk stood. "Well, you boys stay out of trouble, and I'll see you at the next game. One week after this comin' Friday, enit? Yeah, I got a schedule over on the refrigerator." He ambled to the other side of his home. "Yep.

Potlatch. Here. Those logger boys can be pretty rough."

"We'll take care of 'em for you, Uncle," Jesse promised. "When we go to State, we'll get you a ride."

"Good deal. Don't forget everything I told you." Josiah Whitehawk held out his hand and first Jesse and then Sam softly and slowly shook it once.

"Qe'ciyéw'yew', Uncle." Jesse and Sam closed the door behind them and hurried to the pickup. They had a lot of work to do before five o'clock.

12

"I can't go there, Counts."

"Go where, Jesse?"

"To that graveyard. I don't know what's there."

Sam understood. This was too close to home for Jesse. But Sam needed help before everyone showed up. Help from someone who understood his feelings about this discovery of the "lost children's" graveyard. He knew two people who wouldn't think he was crazy to think that ghosts walked those hills.

Sam quickly enlisted Denny and Vicky's help in changing the sledding run. Cindy was home from the University of Idaho for Christmas vacation, and she sat riveted as Sam recounted Josiah Whitehawk's story.

"I knew it!" she exclaimed. "I knew I saw something real walking behind our house at night. Or maybe I should say 'unreal'."

The four chums spent the afternoon smoothing over the old sledding track and creating a new one. The car hood was too heavy for them, but they found an old barrel that worked just as well. Cindy enjoyed playing in the snow again. She missed being with her younger brother and sister.

The new run was even steeper. Before it reached the hackberry grove, it banked sharply toward Denny, Vicky, and Cindy's house. It led straight to the canal. By packing part of the canal with snow, they made a jump over four-and-a-half feet high.

They finished rebuilding the sled run by four o'clock.

"Thanks for doing this, you guys," Sam said. "I gotta go get..."

"Where you think you're going?" Denny asked. "Let's go in for some hot chocolate."

"I'm going to pick up Jessica Whitehawk and come back and go sledding."

"Way to go, man!"

"Yeah, she's cute," Vicky concurred. "Why don't I go with you? She'll be more comfortable. She's pretty shy. We can go get Julia. She and Jessica dance at pow-wows together."

"Okay, thanks. That sounds good. I wasn't sure what to talk about."

"I'll see you later, then, Lover Boy," teased Denny, and Cindy and he went inside.

When Sam drove up with Vicky and Julia, Jessica and her mom were waiting in their long gravel driveway. Seeing Julia, Jessica's mother gave Jessica permission to go with the older high school students. "Be back by ten," Jessica's mom said as Sam backed the pickup around.

The four teenagers squeezed into the pickup cab. Sam was relieved that Vicky got in the passenger's side first. It might have been awkward to sit that closely by Jessica so soon, but Vicky was like a sister to Sam. Vicky and Julia talked a few minutes about who was going to the Winter Dance together as Sam and Jessica listened silently. Then Julia asked Jessica if she was going to the upcoming pow-wow in Nespelem, Washington. The girls discussed their plans until they arrived at the sledding hill.

A group of 12 teens stood near the corner of the old cavalry stables as the four approached. Jesse was quieter than usual, but Sam and he exchanged a brief nod and smiled. Everything was cool.

"How come you guys changed it?" Luke asked.

"Our dads looked at it and thought somebody might get hurt if they crashed into the barn," Sam fibbed.

"Could be, could be..."

"Check out this jump," Denny chimed in to change the subject. The group walked to the bottom of the sled run where it ended at the canal.

"Excellent!" Luke proclaimed, and the subject of the sledding hill change was closed.

For Sam, though, the history of the old location stayed on his mind. They had walked on graves, he couldn't help but remember. He watched Sonny and Julia closely. He was still expecting something bad to happen when he heard Julia scream.

The sled-run builders forgot one thing: the alley near the bottom of the hill behind Denny's house. Denny and Vicky's father sometimes parked behind their house, and he was driving there now. His eyes focused on the icy path ahead, his radio tuned to a Christmas song on the station from Lewiston, he did not see Sonny, mid-air, heading straight toward him.

Suddenly the car skidded sideways into a snow bank. The teenagers ran to the road as Sonny and his paper sled slid in front of Mr. Smith's car and came to a stop.

"What was that?!" Denny's father jumped out of the car. "What are you guys doing?!" he yelled. "This is really dangerous! I didn't see Sonny at all! I almost hit him!" He paused, and his voice trailed off. "But then it was like something took over the brake..."

"Long Shadow!" everyone gasped.

"Yeah, well, you guys should put something across the road if you're going sledding. Denny, you shoulda thought of that."

"Sorry, Dad. We'll put that barrel in the middle of the road where the alley starts."

"Good. I want you to have fun, but you all need to be more careful." Mr. Smith was calming down.

"Okay," the group responded together and headed back up the hill. There was time for one more run before Sam and the girls took Jessica home. Suddenly Sam stopped and turned to Vicky.

"Where's Jessica?" he whispered. They looked back toward the road. There she stood. Alone. They rushed back.

"Jessica, are you alright?" Vicky asked, clutching Jessica's shaking hands. Silently, wide-eyed, Jessica faced Sam and Vicky.

"Wh-what?"

"Did you see Sonny almost get hit?" Sam asked. Jessica looked to Vicky and back to Sam. "Did you see what happened?" Sam repeated.

"Uh..." Jessica started.

"Where were you?"

"I...I was right here," Jessica muttered.

"Umm...okay..." Sam managed to say. "So...do you want to go down the hill again?"

Jessica's eyes cleared. She smiled weakly. "Uh...I...don't feel too good. Can I go home?"

"Sure," Vicky answered.

"Thanks." Jessica walked toward Sam's pickup. Behind her, Sam and Vicky exchanged glances. "Long Shadow," Vicky mouthed. Sam nodded.

"Yes...something weird definitely happened. But something good, not bad," thought Sam as he neared his pickup. He glanced toward the old grave site. "What next?" he wondered.

13

January 1972

Sam couldn't wait for the second half of the basketball season to resume. He guessed he would sub-in mid-first-quarter against Potlatch. Sam was a true sixth man, playing any of three positions. Besides solid rebounding (Josiah Whitehawk will be so impressed!), Sam could also provide valuable 'second-chance' points.

Sam's emergence energized his friend Luke. Teams sagging back to stop Mike around the basket left outside shots open. Coach McNeese needed all the shooters he could get.

Again, Mike was a big help. He grew up around basketball. He immediately detected that sometimes Luke twisted his body when he jumped. They retooled his shot until he was downright deadly from 'downtown.'

The other reserves felt rejuvenated, too.

Like Sam, the boys were lean and farm-strong from bucking bales, picking rock, and building grain bins. Junior was more. And he could be half ornery. In summer he rode broncs, following in the footsteps of his great, great-grandfather, the legendary Nez Perce cowboy Jackson Sundown. He resolved to show Coach McNeese just how tough he could be.

"Nobody pushes us around," Junior pledged. "When Coach needs an enforcer, I'm his man."

Jimmy Redjacket, a member of the Seneca tribe back east, was perhaps the best athlete on the team. To see it, you needed only watch him hoop dance. For 20 minutes, in step with the rapid pounding of war-dance drums, he wove himself through hoop after hoop, until seven interlocked into an intricate, dazzling pattern.

"Coach needs to see what I can do on defense," Jimmy decided. Come mid-January's rematch with Latah Valley, Coach McNeese could keep fresh legs on Harper.

Terry Gibson, the quiet white sophomore guard, was still getting used to his older teammates. The son of the minister at rural Cottonwood Creek Community Church, his teammates' often raunchy language made him blush. Terry started the season on the junior varsity, but after scoring 36 points against Troy, it was obvious he belonged on the varsity.

Terry was smooth as silk, but he hesitated to score in practice. Would they think he was showing them up? What would they do? The first time he put a quick jab-step on Billy and finished with a reverse lay-up, the other players froze. Then this:

"Billy, where's your jock, man? I think it's back where you last saw Terry," Jesse razzed.

"You got took, enit?" Junior joined in.

Billy strode toward Terry with clenched teeth. Terry backed toward the locker room door. Coach McNeese held the ball and moved toward the two boys. Billy suddenly broke out in a wide grin.

"You been holding out us, man! What took you so long?! Sweet move! Lay some skin on me!" Terry shyly gave Billy one of the up-and-down fist taps the boys always did.

"From now on," Terry thought, smiling, "I'm just playing my game." He belonged.

14

Coach McNeese was, shall we say, a tad bit too-into-control. Every day he washed the boys' practice jerseys: blue ones for the first string, white for the second string. School colors. It had been his way for all 21 years of his coaching career. Doing laundry gave him time to think.

As he folded the clean shirts, he thought how surprising this year's squad has been. "Luke's turned into a heckuva shooter. He needs to be on the floor with Denny and Sonny, let them find their spots. Jimmy and Terry both need to play with Billy, see him run the offense. I'd like to see how Junior..."

Coach McNeese stopped folding. The old shirts weren't going to work anymore. He picked up the phone, called Herb's Sporting Goods in Lewiston, and ordered ten blue and white reversible practice jerseys.

15

Sam couldn't tell if Jessica liked him. When he tried to catch her eye in Band, she hid behind her music stand. After Sam put away his trombone at the end of class, he asked Jessica what she did the rest of the week after the sledding party. She just whispered, "Nothing," and fled with her friends.

Sam had to know more. Julia was with Jessica a lot pow-wow dancing. He'd get Julia to find out if Jessica said anything about him.

Sam saw Julia in the hall after practice on Wednesday.

"Jessica said she had fun sledding and that you're really nice. That's a lot for Jessica to say, Counts. I think you're in there, man."

On Thursday, Sam waited by the clarinet case storage spaces before Band. "I'm gonna say this," he coaxed himself.

Jessica walked into the Band Room and saw Sam standing by her clarinet case. She gave Sam a slight smile as she walked toward him.

"A bunch of people go to Ervono's after home games. You want to ask if you can go on Friday?"

Sam blurted out. "We could go in Mike's car with Julia and Sonny and Vicky." Six people in the car would mean one couple couldn't sit together, but Sam knew a bigger group would be better right now. Besides, Jessica's mom might not want her to go with just one other girl and two older white boys, he thought. Mrs. Whitehawk seemed pretty traditional.

"I'd like to go," Jessica replied quietly, at last looking up at Sam. "Should I bring some money?"

"You don't have to," Sam answered and added to himself, "because it's called a *date*."

"Okay."

Sam waited until Jessica walked toward the clarinet section chairs on the stage before he let himself smile. Friday was going to be awesome.

16

Lapwai Wildcats Versus Potlatch Loggers
January 7, 1972

Sam easily spotted Jessica in the pep band front row. A beaded barrette of an eagle in flight held back her long hair. He caught Jessica's eye and grinned. She shyly smiled back and started to wave, but a friend sitting next to her grabbed her arm, and the two girls giggled together. "Sophomores," Sam shrugged.

Mr. Groves shouted, "The Beat Goes On!" and the musicians clipped the Sonny and Cher hit onto the small music holders attached to their horns.

Sam was already fired up about playing real minutes against Potlatch. Seeing Jessica, he was soaring during warm-ups. Sam dribbled left-handed along the baseline and dropped the ball over the rim. He was careful to keep his hand away from the hoop. Coach McNeese? Not too happy giving Potlatch free-throws and possession of the ball to start the game because a player touched the rim. Moving to the rebound side, he lined up behind Denny.

"Counts, when you're in, watch for a lob, enit? I'll be looking for you."

In a few minutes, players and fans stood for the national anthem. The Potlatch starting five was introduced to polite applause. Then the first seven notes of the school song brought the crowd to their feet for the introduction of the Wildcat starting line-up.

The five seniors, with a perfect nine wins, zero losses record, loped out to center court one-by-one as their names were announced. "I'll be out there soon," Sam thought.

It happened more quickly than he expected. Just four minutes gone, the Wildcats already led 12-0. "Sam!" Coach McNeese yelled over the crowd noise. Sam ran to the scorers' table. "Go in for Mike. Let's see some rebounds."

"Number 43 in for Number 41," Sam hollered at Eldon, the school janitor, who also kept the official game statistics for home games.

"You don't have to say who you're going in for, Sammy," Eldon laughed. "Have fun."

Soon, the buzzer sounded and the referee waved Sam in.

"Mike!" Sam shouted. Mike grabbed Sam as they passed.

"Hold on! You got 23, Sam. Go get 'em, man."

Billy set up the offense. "Two!" he shouted. On this play, Sam cut across the key and set a screen for Denny. He wasn't thinking of anything but getting both feet planted for a clean pick when he felt the basketball hit him on the shoulder and watched it roll out of bounds.

"You had him beat, Counts. Look around... I'll hit you on that when you're open," Billy explained as they ran back on defense.

Sam looked toward the bench. Coach McNeese touched an index finger to the corner of his eye. "Look up," he mouthed. Sam nodded back.

The Logger point guard, seeing a somewhat flustered sub in the game, bounce-passed to Number 23. Sam poked at the ball from behind. The referee underneath the basket blew his whistle.

"Reaching in!" he shouted and pointed to Sam. "Number 43."

"23" made both free throws. Coach McNeese called time-out.

"Great start! Let's work on our new play. Sam, you remember what to do?" Sam nodded, wide-eyed. Coach McNeese turned to him. "You're doing fine. Just settle down a little. Remember to move your feet on defense. Don't reach... All right, let's keep this going!"

The horn sounded. Luke slapped Sam on the back. "No worries, Counts," Luke assured him. The Wildcats quickly gathered at mid-court.

"All the way to State, enit?!" They looked at Sam.

"Be ready, Counts," Denny grinned.

"Okay." It was good to know his teammates were behind him. A turnover and one foul. Big deal.

Billy dribbled down-court and passed to Denny. On the back side, Sam fought for rebound position. But instead of handing the ball back to Billy brushing past him, Denny faced the basket, the ball above his head. Denny's eyes caught Sam's, and he tilted his head upwards once.

Sam forgot about his two mistakes. This was exactly where he should be, with four friends he'd known all his life, doing exactly what he should be doing.

And Number 23 forgot about Sam.

The ball left Denny's hand the same time Sam's feet left the floor. It was a perfect lob, six inches off the rim and about eight inches above it.

"Crap, too high," thought Denny. But Sam's right hand met the ball at the top of his jump and softly cradled it.

Sam didn't plan on dunking it. His hand was inside the rim before he could pull it back. He grabbed the rim coming down, and the backboard shook.

The crowd went crazy. The bench leapt to their feet and high-fived each other. The baseline referee blew his whistle, waved both hands above his head, and shouted, "No basket!" The Wildcats didn't care.

Sam struggled not to beam when he looked over to Coach McNeese, who was shaking his head. He waved Sam over after the Logger captain sank the two free throws for the technical foul.

Coach McNeese reluctantly smiled. "Just this once... Remember, now you got two fouls on you."

Ray McNeese stuck to his plan, playing all ten players in various combinations. Luke confidently hit two bombs in the second quarter and two more in the third. The bench played-out the game against Potlatch's exhausted starters falling further behind. Final score: 67 to 42.

9:45 PM

The Wildcat varsity starting five could probably all have fit in the back seat of Mike's family's 1970 Chevrolet Caprice. Two couples could have sat together. Still, Jessica sat by the window next to Julia in the front seat, while Sam sat in the back with Sonny and Vicky. Even with the others chattering about the night and Sonny's eight-track tape of James Brown blaring, Jessica rode silently as they drove along the Clearwater River to Lewiston.

Maybe Lapwai kids liked Ervono's because it was on the edge of Lewiston nearest Lapwai. Maybe it was the excellent pizza. Ervono's was a welcoming place for the groups of white and Indian teens who congregated there after high school events. They sat in booths or played pool or foosball, laughing together.

Except Terry, all Sam's teammates were there. Junior especially was in a good mood. In 19 minutes of play, he got 11 rebounds. He owned the boards. He told hysterical stories of spotlighting deer with the Johnson brothers.

A lot of teenagers could jam into Ervono's wide booths. Sam and Jessica sat together, sharing the medium-sized combination pizza Sam ordered. It seemed every other minute someone got up and somebody else sat down next to them. Sam and Jessica kept getting squeezed together. "Perfect," thought Sam.

They finished eating and joined Julia and Mike at the foosball table where Sonny and Vicky were playing.

"Wanna play?" Vicky asked.

"I don't know how," Jessica answered.

"I bet Counts will show you. But maybe you should start out up front," Julia suggested.

Sam and Jessica took their spots opposite Sonny and Vicky. Sam reached around Jessica to show her how the plastic hockey men slid back and forth on metal rods.

"You'll get it," he assured her.

It was hilarious. Nobody was very good. The only scores came when a defender flailed at the ball creeping toward the goal and bonked it in. They didn't bother to keep score. Jessica was smiling and having fun.

After the game, Jessica realized, "I probably need to go home." They gathered their travel companions and walked toward the parking lot. Jessica paused. "Oh, I left something. I'll see you at the car."

As the group walked toward Mike's car, they heard shouts from the side of the building. Junior was heading toward them in his red pickup. Four boys hooky-bobbed on the icy parking lot, holding the sides of the truck bed and sliding on their feet.

Suddenly Billy hit a manhole cover and lost his footing. Before Junior could do anything, the rear wheels neared Billy's legs under the moving pickup. As his friends watched, frozen in place, Billy was, somehow, standing inches from the passing truck.

"One second you're on the ground, the next second you're standing here!" Jimmy exclaimed.

"Yeah, I know! It was Long Shadow all the way. It felt like somebody grabbed me."

The kids looked at each other. No one was that close to Billy when he fell, and nobody could have reacted so quickly. Sam remembered the last time he heard someone say "Long Shadow" on an icy road.

The five started toward Mike's car.

"Wait!" Sam shouted. "Where's Jessica? She missed everything. I'll go find her." Sam walked back inside Ervono's, but she was nowhere to be seen.

10:40 PM

Sam stepped back outside and saw Jessica standing by Mike's car.

"Where were you?" he asked her.

"I...was just right out here," she stammered.

Sam was baffled. "I didn't see you." She glowered at him.

Jessica had no idea where she was.

She turned without answering and started toward the front seat, but Vicky was already opening the front passenger-side door. She gave Sam a sly smile. For the moment, Jessica's disappearing act was forgotten.

Sam and Jessica slid into the back seat next to Sonny. On the other side, Denny was getting in.

"Can I get a ride to my house?" he asked Mike.

"How come?"

"Lootz wants to cruise around. I just wanna go home."

"Well, yeah. Sure."

The four teens squeezed in the back seat, and Mike drove east to Lapwai. Everyone was tired. For once, even Julia and Vicky sat together quietly. Soon, Denny leaned his head against the window and fell asleep. Mike put on an eight-track of Roberta Flack. Sam's head drooped, and his eyes closed. Next to him, Jessica did the same. A few miles later, she rested her head on Sam's shoulder.

"Why not?" Sam thought, and he placed his right hand down between Jessica and himself. In the car's darkness he soon felt her fingers against his.

17

"Tonight was like the best night ever," Sam thought, lying in bed. "What the heck's bugging me?"

The events at the end of the evening played in his head. First, Billy 'magically' gets pulled out from underneath Junior's moving pickup. Then, when he goes back inside Ervono's to get Jessica, Poof! She appears at Mike's car. Disappearing and reappearing. Like magic.

Out of nowhere, it hit him. "Like a ghost."

"It was like that when we were sledding, too. Where was she when Sonny almost got hit by Denny's dad?"

"*But then it was like something took over the brake,*" Mr. Smith had said. Then, all of a sudden, Jessica was standing by the side of the road, alone.

"Did anyone see her when that was all happening?" Sam wondered.

"When did this all start?"

The knife. Sam had forgotten about it. He got out of bed, opened the top drawer of his dresser, and held it in the palm of his hand. The bone handle reflected the streetlight. It was so weird how it just disappeared in Mrs. Preston's classroom and then reappeared on the sledding hill eight years later, Sam thought. Not just laying somewhere on the ground, but put somewhere, somewhere safe, where he could find it. Someplace special.

A place he wasn't supposed to be. Josiah Whitehawk's only request was to stay away from the graves on the hill. Sam was now wide awake.

"Are there ghosts there?"

11:55 PM

"No way I'm gonna fall back asleep now." Sam put on the clothes lying in a heap at the foot of his bed, slid the knife into his pocket, and carried his old basketball sneakers as he inched his way downstairs. He slipped out the back door into the half-light of the vacant street.

Sam found himself walking south on a well-worn trail along the bottom of the hill. As the path joined the long-forgotten canal near the old one-story brick building where he went to grade school, he slowed and circled the building. Just then, he saw the movements of shadows silhouetted against the walls of Room Five. Sam stood, frozen.

"Sometimes they leave and walk to the graveyard. Their shadows stay behind." Vicky was standing under a chestnut tree, hidden just out of the light.

"Vicky, what are you doing here?!" Sam cried out.

"Same thing you're doing, Sammy. Thinking about how it all fits together. Sonny and Billy. Jessica. The knife. Yeah, I was wondering where Jessica was when Billy fell under Junior's pickup, too." Sam and Vicky watched the shadows chase each other across the room. "They'll lie down pretty soon," Vicky explained.

"Chize, Vicky, how many times have you seen them before?!" For the moment, Jessica was forgotten.

"Lots of times, Counts. Cindy saw them first behind our house. Remember? Then one night I saw them. Walking. Cindy wouldn't let me go then, but when she went to college, I snuck out and followed them. One of them saved Sonny, then Billy. One of them took your knife, Sammy. I don't know why she gave it back."

"She?"

"I guess I just think of them as girls, like me. It would be so sad to have to leave home and be forgotten."

"I never thought about that."

"Girls think about different stuff than guys. We think about our friends in different ways. We think about them when we're alone. We give each other things to remember each other by. I know you and Denny..."

"Do you think he knows about the knife?" Sam interrupted. He felt guilty he didn't share his secret with Denny...it was just so easy to talk to Vicky.

"Yeah, he knows," Vicky answered. "Anyway, like I was saying, you and Denny used to give each other Christmas presents when you were little, but you don't do that anymore. Julia and I still do."

"I bet Jessica and her friends give each other things."

"You're thinking about her, huh? She's cool. Yeah, they give each other bells and feathers and beadwork for their pow-wow dresses, Julia told me. They're tight."

"That's cool. I know everything they wear at pow-wows has a lot of meaning. Jimmy told us about his stuff last year at the E-Peh-Tes⁸ pow-wow at the Pi-Nee-Waus."

"Julia told me some things she wears are over a hundred years old," Vicky added. "Elders keep memories and traditions alive by handing them down. Everything has a story."

The night air was chilly. As Sam put his hands in his pockets, he felt the small Barlow knife. He took it out and watched the streetlight strike the luminescent handle.

"What's the story of your knife, I wonder?"

"There's one way to find out," Sam replied.

---

⁸ (*Ipéetes*) Ē\pə\täs

18

January 8, 1972

To Sam, everything about Aunt Milly's home felt old. But a good old, like stepping back in time. A wedding portrait in an ornate oval frame of her parents, both gone for the past two years, commanded the front room. The plant-dye colors of the corn husk bag draped over Aunt Milly's overstuffed chair had faded into soft pastels. A photograph of turn-of-the-century Lapwai showed almost as many tepees as wood frame cabins and houses.

Even the quietness felt old, and to Sam, comforting. An old black-and-white television, in a huge cabinet, served mostly to hold a dozen high school graduation pictures displayed in their bi-fold frames, each message beginning "To Auntie..." Sam had never seen the television actually turned on. He wondered if it worked.

All this he saw through the front door window pane. He heard the deep echo of each second's click of the fireplace mantel clock. Aunt Milly's moccasin-muffled footsteps scuffed the wooden floor as she made her way to the front door.

"Redwing, I'm so happy to see you! Come in and have a piece of pie." Sam was not disappointed. He was again nine years old, coming in from a day of roaming the hills with Gordy.

"Thank you, Auntie. I'm sorry I haven't come for a while."

"You've been busy. You been a good boy?"

"Of course, Auntie. I don't want to get in trouble with you," Sam said as they embraced.

The apprehension Sam felt regarding what to talk about with Aunt Milly disappeared. It was always like this: he would have a piece of pie, tell Aunt Milly how his folks were, and assure her that he was doing well in school. Then, for the next three hours, Aunt Milly would tell Sam stories...about her life in Oregon, about when she was a young girl...

Today she told Sam about a basketball trip she took to Kendrick in high school. As the rickety old bus crept up the hill near where Potlatch Creek entered the Clearwater, the girls jumped out the back door of the bus, ran to the top of the hill, and waited there for the bus to finally arrive.

"Oh, that bus driver was so mad," Aunt Milly said, with laughter in her voice. "By the way, I heard the Wildcats are pretty good this year."

"We're undefeated, Auntie. I'm getting to play a lot."

"Well, you're tall enough. We had real tall boys when I was in school, too." Aunt Milly's voice trailed off as she remembered a time long past. After a few moments she was back with Sam.

"I'd like to go see you boys. Maybe I can get a ride."

"I'll talk to my mom," Sam promised. "She could probably pick you up. We have a game here this Friday."

"That would be real good."

Sam and Aunt Milly sat quietly. The clock counted out the seconds before Sam broke the silence.

"Say, Auntie, I brought something I wanted to show you. I was wondering if you could tell me something about it." Sam reached into his pocket and pulled out his knife.

Milly Lawyer's face went ashen. The clock sounded deafening as she sat stricken with a look of deep grief. Tears welled in her eyes.

Sam was horrified. He would never hurt his Auntie for anything in the world. He recalled when Gordy gave him the knife. Now, eight years later, he realized for the first time the knife was not Gordy's to give.

There was more than that in Aunt Milly's face, though: something much deeper than the innocent transgressions of two nine-year-olds. Sam strained to hear Aunt Milly's voice as she whispered to herself, "I never gave the knife back to May."

Finally, Aunt Milly managed to softly ask Sam, "Redwing, how did you get this knife?"

"Auntie, I'm so sorry I took it. Gordy and I found it upstairs when we were playing, and he gave it to me for my birthday," Sam answered, his voice breaking.

"That's okay, Sammy. You and Gordy didn't know." Aunt Milly paused again as her memories took her back.

"I had that knife when I was just a girl, even younger than you are now. I had a friend from the Oregon reservation who came to the tuberculosis hospital. She was really sick. We were best friends. We told each other many secrets. We never kept anything from each other. Her name was May. The knife was a gift from her brother. I was supposed to give it back to her when she got better and was ready to go home. She didn't get better. She always wanted to go home to her family real bad. She told me the first thing she was going to do when she got home was to say to her brother, 'I'm ready to go fishin', enit?' She really wanted to take her knife back with her to Warm Springs." Aunt Milly sighed. "I was so sad, I forgot all about the knife. I watched my father bury her."

"On the hill behind the horse barn?" He already knew the answer.

Aunt Milly's eyes met Sam's, surprised. "Yes. How do you know about that?"

"Josiah Whitehawk told me and Jesse Waters about the graveyard. We went to ask him if we could go sledding there."

"I hope you kids stayed away from the graves." Sam lowered his eyes and nodded. Aunt Milly continued. "I had lots of friends at the hospital. Some went home. Some didn't. This is the first I thought about them in a long time. Do you want to see a picture of May?"

"Yes, Auntie, I'd really like to see a picture of your friend."

Aunt Milly started to rise. Sam jumped up, and holding her by the arm, helped her stand.

"I keep my pictures upstairs," she explained.

Sam waited as Aunt Milly crossed the living room, dining room, and kitchen to the stairway at the back of the house. He could hear Auntie hobble upstairs, and he imagined her carefully grasping the handrail. She paused several seconds before tackling the next step. Finally, she reached the top.

As Aunt Milly searched through boxes of photographs, Sam walked over to the graduation pictures on the television cabinet.

There were many from other towns on Indian reservations- Wellpinit, Fort Hall, Saint Ignatius.... Several, though, were of kids Sam knew. He picked up a picture of Billy, wearing the beaded medallion he often wore on game days. Sam smiled, remembering Coach McNeese's first days in Lapwai.

"That seems like a long time ago," Sam thought. Then he reminded himself, "I gotta remember to mail my picture to Auntie." Just as Sam put Billy's picture back in place, Aunt Milly returned from upstairs.

"Here it is." She handed Sam a large group photograph. "It's a good picture. May and them are all in front of the hospital. She's right there, the tall girl in the back."

Sam stared at the girl with waist-length hair Aunt Milly indicated. Looking straight at the camera was Jessica Whitehawk.

"Chize!" Vicky exclaimed. "What did you do after you saw the picture?"

"I kinda freaked out," Sam admitted. "I told Auntie I had to go to practice and took off," Sam answered. They sat outside Vicky's house in Sam's pickup. He called her right after he left Aunt Milly's house. He needed someone to talk to.

"You didn't give her the knife?" quizzed Vicky.

"Crap! I shoulda done that, huh?"

Vicky rolled her eyes. "You think?" She continued. "You didn't ask her anything?"

"Like what?"

"Like what?! Like, 'What was May's last name?' 'What was her brother's name?' You gotta ask questions if we're going to figure this out, Counts. Here, give me some paper." Vicky tore out a sheet from Sam's Biology II notebook and pulled out the pencil slid into the wire binder.

"Okay, Number One: 'What's May's last name?' Number Two: 'What's her brother's name?' Number Three: 'What's...'"

"Number Three: 'Does Aunt Milly know the Whitehawks'?" Sam interrupted.

"Number Three: 'Is Sam the worst detective ever?' Of course she knows the Whitehawks, Counts. It's Lapwai. Everybody knows everybody."

"I mean," Sam explained, "does she know the family very well? Like maybe Jessica's mom is Warm Springs, or her grandmother, or something."

"Good idea. I got it," Vicky said as she recorded Question Number Three.

"Question Four... I don't know Question Four yet. I gotta think about it. I'll call you."

"Okay. Hey, thanks, Sis. I wouldn't know what to do without you."

"Obviously. I can't always take care of you, Counts," teased Vicky.

"I'll see you tomorrow." Sam folded the List of Questions paper twice and stuffed it in his shirt pocket.

"I need to think about it, too," Sam replied. And he needed to go back and see Aunt Milly.

January 9, 1972

Aunt Milly was expecting Sam. She answered his knock on the door with a light in her eyes.

"I was thinking I'd see you today, Redwing." Aunt Milly gestured to the couch next to her chair. "I'll go get some pie."

"Thanks, Auntie," Sam replied. "Do you want some help?"

"Oh, no, I think I can still handle this."

Sam sat down and listened to the mantel clock's heavy ticking. He still carried Vicky's List of Questions in his shirt pocket. Soon, Aunt Milly brought out a large slice of lemon meringue pie.

"I made Gordy's favorite today, just for the heck of it."

"How's he doing?"

"Oh, he's the top of his class," Aunt Milly boasted. "He studies real hard. He wants to go into law enforcement, just like his grandpa." Sam glanced at the photograph of Corbett Lawyer on the fireplace mantel. Beside it lay his tribal police badge.

Gordy's mother remarried when he was 11, and they moved to Umatilla, Oregon. She became very busy with Indian water rights, traveling throughout the Northwest. Gordy went with her as often as possible. Gordy and Sam didn't see each other in the summers after that.

"That's great. Did he send you a graduation picture yet?"

"No, not yet. How about you? Or did you flunk out?" A smile snuck onto Aunt Milly's face.

"No, I think I'll make it."

"Good."

After a short pause, Sam began. "Anyway, I came over to tell you that Mom can pick you up for the game this Friday. Do you want to go to the JV game?"

"Oh yes, I probably know some of those younger boys. I don't get around much, but I still want to see you kids. I don't want to just be stuck in the past."

"Do you remember a lot of people from way back?"

Aunt Milly studied Sam for a long moment. Finally, she said, "I know you didn't just come to tell me about going to the basketball game. When you looked at the picture I showed you last time, you turned white. I mean *whiter*," Auntie joked.

Sam smiled. "I know. I'm sorry I left so fast. That picture of your friend kinda shook me up. May looked just like a friend of mine."

"Who's that, Sammy?"

"You know Josiah Whitehawk's granddaughter Jessica?"

"Oh, yes. She's learning all the old dances. I go over to the Buildin' and help out sometimes. Get that picture from the cupboard, would you, Redwing? I left it down here so I could look at it some more." Sam brought the large group photograph of the children at Fort Lapwai Tuberculosis Sanatorium to Aunt Milly. Together they pondered the resemblance between May and Jessica.

"Jessica really does look like May," Milly Lawyer agreed. She pictured Jessica's perfect face and remembered May. "All the boys liked her. She was real pretty until..." Aunt Milly couldn't bring herself to think of all the things tuberculosis stole from May. A moment later she exclaimed, "Oh, I see! So Jessica Whitehawk's got your eye?"

"Yeah, I guess I kinda like her, Auntie," Sam admitted. "We've sorta gone out a couple of times."

"A couple of times? That's good. She's real shy."

"I know. Sometimes I don't know what to talk about with her."

"I don't think you have to talk very much."

"Good."

After a long, thoughtful pause, Aunt Milly probed. "Was there something else, Sammy?" Once again, Sam marveled at Aunt Milly's wisdom.

"It's about the knife, Auntie. I'm not the only one to have it the last eight years." Sam slowly described 'losing' the knife in fourth grade, 'finding' it again a few weeks ago, and the incidents with Sonny and Billy.

"Both times Jessica seemed to just disappear."

Aunt Milly's eyes penetrated the photograph resting on her lap. Sam waited silently as Aunt Milly thought. At one point, she closed her eyes. Several minutes later, she spoke.

"It's May, Redwing. She's following you and your friends. She wants you to take the knife to her brother."

Both the pie and the List of Questions were forgotten.

19

December 10, 1971
A Month Earlier

Ron Harper, Sr., who everyone called Big Ron, stomped down the bleacher steps moments after Mike sank the final shot of Latah Valley's only loss of the season. He slammed his Ford pickup into reverse, spun gravel as he stormed from the Latah Valley High School gym, and sped home. He swerved down the long gravel driveway, drove on his well-tended lawn, and leapt onto the porch.

In moments, he was on the phone with his sister Janice in Portland. Fifteen minutes later, Big Ron's nephew, six foot six Justin Murphy, a reserve forward on the Benson High School basketball team of the Portland Interscholastic League, was on his way to becoming a Latah Valley Falcon.

December 12, 1971

Luckily for Latah Valley, none of the members of the governing body of the Idaho Interscholastic Activities Association were dry-land wheat farmers. Otherwise, they would know that Ron Harper, Sr. did not really need to have his nephew from

Portland live with them and help out on the family farm. A 3,200 acre farm seemed awfully large to the southern Idahoans who would decide if Latah Valley's hardship case request for Justin Murphy had merit. They didn't know that by even late October all the plowing was finished, the winter wheat was planted, and what straw they needed for the 4-H steers was already baled and in the barn. In December, Big Ron could take his time in the shop replacing broken sickle sections on the combine headers and giving all the machinery a thorough going-over.

Big Ron still knew some people in Boise from his days serving on the Idaho Wheat Commission, and he made a few calls. At two o'clock in the afternoon, the IIAA board met in emergency session. On December 15th, Coach Roy Bradley received a letter from Boise stating that Justin Murphy was cleared to play basketball for the Latah Valley Falcons.

When Big Ron got the call from Coach Bradley, he thanked him for all his work for the young people of Latah Valley and did what he always did when he needed to mull something over: he took the long way to the Grange over Bear Ridge Road.

"Okay, Step One is done. But Justin's got a long way to go to help make sure Lapwai doesn't get away with that again," he thought to himself. Counting the return game down at Lapwai, a probable district championship game in late February, and a possible squaring-off at State, Latah Valley would have to see Lapwai three more times. Big Ron Harper was determined that Lapwai was not going to beat Latah Valley again.

But to Big Ron, Justin was 'soft.' Ron Junior and the other cousins called him City Boy. As he drove along stubbled wheat fields dusted with patches of snow, Big Ron remembered last summer, when Janice brought Justin up from Portland to spend some time getting to know her side of the family and to 'get a taste of farm life.'

His first day hauling hay with Big Ron, Ron Junior, and Ron's friend and teammate Rusty Bush, Justin couldn't hold up his end. Halfway through unloading the 160 bales on the flat-bed hay truck, he took off his gloves and sat down. Big Ron turned off the gas motor on the portable hay elevator.

"What the hell are you doing?!" he shouted.

"I'm tired, Uncle Ron," Justin whined. "It's hot. I need a drink. My gloves are full of hay."

"It's 10:30 in the morning! You think this is hot?! Get a drink and get going!" Big Ron fumed as they finished unloading the truck.

The crew headed back to the alfalfa field, the boys in the back of the truck, Big Ron seething up front. "City Boy's gonna get a taste of farm work today," he snarled to himself.

The crew loaded the truck and headed back to the barn. The breeze from the top of the seven-rows-high load of hay felt good to Justin, but he could feel the day getting hotter.

Back again at the barn, Big Ron pulled the truck alongside the barn's open doorway. Big Ron surprised the boys by saying, "Justin, you're inside the barn this load. The rest of you boys can take a break."

The next 45 minutes were the hardest of Justin's life. Big Ron kept up a barrage of hay bales. As soon as Justin had one bale in place, another was waiting for him. 160 times.

"Slow down!" Justin pleaded.

"You get a rest when we're done, boy. <u>This</u> is what farm work is all about!" Big Ron shouted.

Finally, Justin turned around and saw an empty truck. He collapsed onto a row of bales. Big Ron hopped off the back of the truck.

"You did okay, there, Justin. You just might amount to something someday." To Justin Murphy, Uncle Ron was a scary man. But he never complained about farm work again.

December 17, 1971
Nick Yochum

Now Big Ron had a new challenge for his overgrown nephew. "That McNeese kid's gonna eat Justin alive if I don't do something about it," he thought.

At 8:30 in the morning Big Ron pulled up to the Latah Valley Grange Supply. He walked in for a cup of coffee and to see who he might shoot the breeze with.

"Hey Ron, long time no see," hollered Clint, the co-op manager. "You didn't stick around long after the last game."

"Don't talk to me about that game," grumbled Big Ron as he helped himself to the coffee pot.

Just then, behind Clint, he noticed an enormous, but familiar figure putting packages of combine O-rings on a pegboard rack. It was Nick Yochum, the center on last year's state championship team.

"Hey Clint, wait a sec... What's Nick up to nowadays?"

"Well, he's helping out here for a while. He drove truck for Merritt in harvest, and now he's hoping to get on at the elevator."

"He's not going to school?"

"Nah, Nick's not much for school. You mighta heard the coach down at Lewis-Clark State talked to him about playing there, but Nick, he just wants to stay home. Maybe someday get his own place."

"He still play ball?"

"Yeah, he goes down to Lewiston twice a week. Wants to stay in shape."

"He's put on a little weight," Big Ron commented.

"Yeah. Man muscle," Clint agreed.

Big Ron was getting an idea. He smiled. "Say, Clint, I could use Nick for a couple weeks. I'll cover his wages. How about it?"

"Sure, Ron. No problem." People didn't say no to Big Ron Harper.

"Good. Send him over to the place coupla days after Christmas about eight. Tell him to bring his sweats."

20

December 27, 1971

Justin Murphy hated walking into a room full of strangers. They always stared at him. As he exited Terminal A of the Spokane International Airport, towering over his fellow passengers, he was already in a sour mood. Seeing his uncle Big Ron Harper and his annoying cousin Ron Junior waiting for him at the baggage carrousel didn't help.

"Get your bags, Justin. Let's go."

"Nice to see you, too, Uncle Ron," mumbled Justin under his breath.

Big Ron, Ron Junior, and Justin rode without a word into downtown Spokane for breakfast. After they settled into their booth at Denny's, Big Ron finally broke the silence.

"You know why you're here, Justin?" Big Ron asked.

"I guess so," he replied.

"Well, let's make sure you know so. You're here to win yourself a state championship, son. It's something you'll carry with you the rest of your life. Nobody will be able to take it away from you. No matter what happens, you'll know that at least once in your life you were the best."

Justin looked up from playing with his napkin. Uncle Ron had his full attention.

"For the next two-and-a-half months you'll be part of something bigger than yourself. You don't realize it yet, but you're part of a community, son. Those people up there in the stands, some of them went to school with your mother. They knew your grandma and grandpa. Those people work together and overcome hardships together. You'll be playing for them, Justin. You'll be playing for every Harper who ever worked the land the last 100 years. Does that make sense?"

Justin met his uncle's eyes and nodded.

December 28, 1971

Many barns in America have basketball hoops nailed to walls. Some hoops even have nets. The Harper's barn had a regulation-size hardwood floor, complete with court lines and glass backboards.

Nick showed up a few minutes before eight, met his new protégé, and dressed down. Big Ron explained to Justin.

"Justin, you're about to learn how to play basketball Latah Valley style. We'll start with defense."

When Latah Valley slows opponents and sets up their legendary one-three-one zone, it's as if a wall's erected around the key. Every passing lane is filled.

The big man's job is to see no one touches the ball inside the key.

"You own this piece of the court, Justin. Nobody gets in. Ron and Rusty are going to move the ball around the perimeter, and you're going to keep Nick out of the key. You're facing the ball, but you're watching underneath. Here we go."

Ron passed to his friend on the opposite side of the court. Nick crossed into the key, slammed into Justin, and knocked him on his butt. Ron and Rusty howled.

"What happened, Justin?" Big Ron asked with a smile.

"He can't do that! I had my feet set!"

"Welcome to Idaho, son. Okay, you and Nick switch."

Nick showed Justin how to pick up a big man outside the key with a wide, low stance, his weight forward. He taught him to use his hands on his opponent's back, keeping his elbows in. For the next 45 minutes they went over it and over it. Justin was getting the hang of it.

For the following three mornings Ron, Rusty, Nick, and Justin practiced defense while Big Ron watched. Justin learned how to pick up a man on the baseline, cross in front of him, and 'squeeze' him out of bounds. In the afternoons Ron and Justin had team practice in town.

On Friday they started working on offense. Justin brought his big-city love of outside shooting with him. Big Ron explained to him that each

Falcon had a role. Justin's points were underneath the basket.

"You're the tallest player in the league, son. You should be unstoppable."

Nick showed Justin how to use a drop-step to create space for easy lay-ins. In the middle of the key, Justin developed a soft jump-hook. After six days he was comfortable shooting it with either hand.

The Falcons were reloaded and ready for their rematch with Lapwai.

21

January 11, 1972

"Do you like him?" whispered Jessica.

"What?" Julia turned around. They'd just finished dance practice at the Pi-Nee-Waus and were almost out the front doors.

"Do you like Mike?" Jessica repeated.

Julia paused. "Yeah, I guess I do. We have fun together."

Jessica looked up at Julia and boldly proclaimed, "I like Sam."

Julia smiled. "I know. I can tell."

Jessica's face grew worried. "Really?" Julia nodded.

"Is it okay?"

Julia placed a hand on Jessica's arm and smiled again. "Yeah, it's okay. Sam and Mike are nice. Everybody likes them." Jessica breathed a sigh of relief.

She looked away and said, "I think I want to do something for Sam. Make him something."

"Me, too," Julia replied. "You know, Valentine's Day is comin' up. You wanna make them something together?"

"That would be fun," Jessica answered. "When?" Just then, she got an idea. "This weekend is our encampment up my aunt's place on the Prairie. We do it every year. It's always before the Time for Digging Roots. Ladies only. You wanna come?"

Julia thought a moment. "I promised Vicky we'd hang out."

"She can come, too."

"Cool! She likes doing Indian stuff," Julia grinned. "Almost a real Indi'n, enit?" The girls both laughed.

"So, what should we make?" Jessica wondered.

Jessica's beaded barrette caught Julia's eyes. A plan popped into her head. "You gonna bring your beads?"

Ida Whitehawk filled the back of her wood-paneled station wagon with wool blankets and boxes of groceries. The girls played Keep Away with Jessica's two little sisters a few moments and then piled into the car for the short drive up the Clearwater River to Jessica's aunt's cabin.

Where Four Mile Creek emptied into the Clearwater, a stand of willows and cottonwoods shaded a small sand bar. A narrow turnoff appeared near an overgrown cattle chute, and Ida stopped the car. Jessica hopped out and opened the large metal gate with a Keep Out sign attached with baling wire. They wound their way steeply uphill two-and-a-half miles along a small canyon stream until they reached a summit overlooking the Clearwater. Smoke rose from the stovepipe of a small cabin tucked among several old, gnarled locust trees and from a small fire pit where sweathouse rocks were heating. Three cars were already parked alongside the cabin.

"My cousins from Kamiah beat us here," Jessica announced. She was excited to see her cousins and to share this cherished occasion with her new friends. "I bet the elders are already cooking." Jessica pointed to an ancient tepee. "We'll sleep in the lodge." They lugged bags of clothing, blankets, and sleeping bags inside and stashed them along the deer and elk skin walls.

"We have to leave room for tonight. Everybody meets here for stories." Julia and Vicky smiled and squeezed each other's hands. Vicky bounced on the balls of her feet excitedly as the adventure began.

With a venison stew simmering and fry bread warming on a cast iron wood stove, the older ladies visiting, the little girls chasing each other around the locust trees, the bigger girls gossiping about boys, Jessica, Julia, and Vicky plotted their escape. "We're just going to do some beadwork on my dress," Jessica fibbed to her mother. Ida Whitehawk frowned. "It's a surprise, Mom." Jessica turned on her most beguiling smile.

"Okay...be careful. Be back for dinner," Ida Whitehawk called out after them, and the girls slipped away to start Sam's and Mike's Valentine's Day gifts in secret.

After dinner around a long pine-plank table lined with benches, everyone filed into the tepee and sat in a circle on piles of soft hides around a blazing fire. One-by-one the elders told Coyote stories; often funny at first, then ending with lessons about life. Gradually the fire became a glowing bed of coals, and the girls rolled out their sleeping bags. The women parted with, *"Ta'c kuleewit*[9]...good night 'áyats," and retired to the comfort of soft cots inside the cabin.

That's when the real fun began. The older girls took turns telling stories of the *te'lk k'úcwin*[10], Stick Indians, bad people in life, banished to live in the trees, who come down in the darkest hours to trick the unwary. Finally, when they could no longer stay awake and the fire so low their faces turned to shadows, the girls dropped off.

All except Jessica. Something, someone, haunted her thoughts. When she herself was one of the little girls she loved falling asleep in the tepee, deliciously scared, the comforting warmth of her cousins next to her, the shadows of the rising smoke dancing on the walls. She forced her eyes closed and hoped for the night to take her away. She finally drifted off and dreamed.

---

[9] täts\kə\LAU\it

[10] tə\LIL\ə\kwin

She dreamed of water. And a river, with swift current, calling her name. In her dream, Jessica saw herself clad in her pow-wow dress, once her ancestors' and now in her care, standing beside a riverbank.

She rose and touched the dress, folded on top of her pow-wow suitcase behind her. She slid the heavy dress over her nightgown, put on her dance moccasins, gently lifted the tepee flap, and stepped into the night.

Jessica stopped to listen to the voice chanting inside her head. "Follow the water...follow the water..." She stepped off the road and down a rocky embankment to a well-worn deer trail alongside the canyon stream. In the moonlight, she slowly, carefully, made her way toward the river. "Down the Clearwater, the Snake, and finally, the Columbia. Home." May's home.

Julia suddenly woke. She saw Jessica's empty sleeping bag in the red light of the embers and roused Vicky. Without a sound, they quickly dressed. The girls shivered as they stepped into the brisk night air. Julia signaled, "Wait!" and twirled back to grab two blankets to wrap around their shoulders.

Still silent as the night, they looked at each other. Which way? Somehow they both knew. Together they nodded and followed the road downward to the river.

Forty minutes later, they found her. Already barefoot, Jessica's back was turned to them, and they saw her reach behind to loosen the leather ties of her pow-wow dress. Moonlight reflected off Jessica's shoulders as her dress dropped to the sand and she stepped into the freezing water of the Clearwater.

Julia and Vicky sprang forward, grabbed Jessica by her arms, and pulled her back ashore. She turned toward them with a flash of anger. Her eyes locked on Julia and then Vicky. All at once, a grateful smile spread across her face. Jessica shivered in the cold and melted into the arms of her friends.

Julia removed the blanket from her own shoulders and draped it over Jessica's as Vicky bent to pick up the ancient leather dress. They helped Jessica into her moccasins and made their way back to the warmth of the lodge as quietly as they had come.

Answers would have to wait.

22

January 12, 1972

Between Boise in the south and Coeur d'Alene in the north are some of the most spectacular landscapes in the country. Hells Canyon, along the border with Oregon, is the deepest gorge on the continent. Cutting across central Idaho, the Salmon, the River of No Return, is the longest river in the Lower 48 contained in one state. The Selway-Bitterroot Wilderness Area and the Frank Church-River of No Return Wilderness Area combine to form the country's largest forest preserve outside Alaska. It's a long way from southern Idaho to northern Idaho.

It's easy to see why basketball teams from northern schools usually got little recognition in the newspaper polls. Southern Idaho sportswriters just didn't see the teams up north. But word spread that Lapwai and Latah Valley had maybe the two best big men in the state. All schools. Period.

As the lop-sided scores piled up, Lapwai and Latah Valley rose in the rankings. Two weeks before their highly-anticipated rematch, southeastern Teton and southwestern New Plymouth both lost.

The Wildcats and the Falcons took their places as the number one and number two teams in the state.

23

Friday, January 14, 1972
One Week Before the Game

The Lapwai High School gymnasium was one of the last old-time 'balcony' gyms still in use in Idaho. Opposing coaches hated it. The fans were literally right on top of you. The Falcons dreaded going to Lapwai.

Roy Bradley called Principal Richardson and reasoned that there would be no way everyone who wanted to watch this game could fit in Lapwai's cracker-box gym. Lewis-Clark State College in Lewiston offered their gym, he explained, and both schools could split a tidy gate.

Mr. Richardson knew better than relinquish home-court advantage. "Besides," he thought, "after the treatment we got up there, Latah Valley owes us a visit."

Monday, January 17, 1972
Four Days Before the Game

Mr. Richardson called Coach Bradley at nine in the morning with his plan: advance-ticket sales. Of the 850 gym seats, Latah Valley could have 350.

500 home fans could attend, same as the number on the *Entering Lapwai* sign out on the highway. Everyone else could listen to the game on KRLC, out of Lewiston.

350 Latah Valley folks were in for a surprise.

24

Carl Richardson knew he had an opportunity- a 'teachable moment' they call it in education. He sat at his desk in the principal's office and listened to the kids' hallway chatter between classes. He smiled at the "Aaaaaayyyyyy" they said in unison after each other's jokes. New teachers were always surprised how easily the Indian kids and the white kids laughed together. They were not who they were made out to be.

"What should we do," he thought, "to impact this moment?" He wanted the Latah Valley folks to see what he saw every day. Pride. Tradition. Harmony.

Just then Coach Evans tapped on the open office door.

"Carl, you got a minute? Could you sign...?"

"Hey, Jeff..." Principal Richardson interrupted. "When did you first 'get' Lapwai?" Sam's father knew exactly what Carl Richardson meant. He sat across from the Principal's Desk and thought a moment. Then he smiled.

"It was our first year here. Carol and I were invited to the pow-wow held in the spring at the Pi-

Nee-Waus. They gave us front row seats at half-court. Place of honor. Lots of parents came over to thank us for coming, then we were invited to join the round dance." Jeff paused. "How come?"

Carl thought out-loud. "You know, a pow-wow and a basketball game are similar in some ways. They both start with ceremonies that..."

"You're going to use this game for something, aren't you?"

"Plan to," Carl admitted. "You know, people don't really know Lapwai."

Jeff nodded. "Go on, Carl..."

"At a pow-wow, Indian veterans present the state and national flags. Somebody carries a wooden staff with eagle feathers on top for the various tribes..."

"Okay..." Jeff Evans jumped in. "First, a Nez Perce war vet places the American flag..."

"But we don't play the national anthem right away... At pow-wows there are some speakers first. We welcome Latah Valley...as our guests... Reverend Matthews would be good at that...first in Nez Perce...yeah! I like that. Then in English...a message of friendship," he continued.

"Then the national anthem...no, not yet... We need something that shows honor...true sportsmanship, right? The way the Nez Perce honor elders."

"But who?" Jeff wondered. "Someone who always..." The answer hit Mr. Richardson immediately.

"...Always sits in the same front row seat, center court, his big hat in his lap. Josiah Whitehawk." Jeff reached across the big oak desk and gave Carl one of the up-and-down taps of the fist they'd seen the kids do in the halls a thousand times. They laughed.

"How can we thank Mr. Whitehawk for his many years of support?" Carl wondered, getting back to business.

"Easy! A lifetime season pass. And free popcorn for his hat," Jeff laughed.

"But we need something as soon as Latah Valley folks come in." Mr. Richardson's thoughts returned to pow-wows. "At a pow-wow, right away you hear dancers' bells. You hear drums. We need <u>that</u>. War-dance drums over the PA."

"I like it, Carl," Jeff agreed. "I'd like to stay and talk some more with you about this, but I gotta get back to class." Principal Richardson scratched his signature on the football equipment requisition forms for the coming season, and Coach Evans left him to finalize plans for Friday night.

Mr. Richardson wandered the empty halls. He heard teachers' voices and the scraping of chair legs on the wooden classroom floors. The school's old public address system wouldn't work for what he had in mind: too faint in some places, too loud in others.

"We need speakers everywhere in the gym area- entryway, halls, even bathrooms," he thought. "This

Friday, our friends from Latah Valley are going to know they're in Indian Country."

Tuesday, January 18, 1972
3:15 PM
Three Days Before the Game
Mr. Barrett and Mr. Turner

Mr. Barrett and Mr. Turner sat across the conference table from Mr. Richardson in his office.

"Fellas, I got you subs for the next two days." They looked at each other, surprised. "I think you'll like what I have planned for you."

Bob Barrett was the shop teacher, but his true passion was furniture making. He also did remodeling during the summer. He loved the classic architecture of Lapwai High School. Over the last ten years he built several Craftsman-style trophy cases for the school and two summers ago remodeled a storage room into a counselor's office for Reverend Matthews.

Everett Turner taught four sessions of Chemistry each day, but every spring he offered his favorite course, Electronics. He was an avid amateur radio operator. A large man, Mr. Turner had a little bounce in his step showing students the latest electronic gadget.

Mr. Richardson explained to his carpenter and his electrician his plan to outfit the gym, adjacent hallways, and bathrooms with a top-rate sound system.

"Whatever you need, buy." He handed each teacher an envelope with signed blank checks. "You won't have to do any sub plans. Your classes will both meet in the library for a two-day research project." All at once, the two teachers grew concerned for the high school's elderly librarian. "Don't worry, she'll have plenty of help," Carl Richardson assured them.

"Show up anytime tomorrow," Mr. Richardson continued. "Get whatever you need in Lewiston. If you need coupla boys to help, just let me know. They will be excused from their regular schoolwork. You need Vernon to get you a ladder or anything, just holler. He knows this project is his top priority for the next two days."

Bob and Everett were like boys again. They couldn't wait to get started. They were antsy to finish their meeting with Mr. Richardson, get downstairs to the gym, and take measurements.

Sitting in the middle of the conference table was a small plastic box. Mr. Richardson stretched forward and flipped it over. The cover on the cassette tape case read "The Rapid River Boys." The photograph under the title showed eight Nez Perce men around a war-dance drum, their drumsticks raised in their right hands. Each drummer's left hand pressed on his knee. They leaned slightly forward, their braids dangling freely, heads tilted back to hit the high notes of a war-dance chant crescendo.

"Three days from now, fellas, 350 of our closest Latah Valley friends are going to be introduced to the traditional sounds of The Rapid River Boys."

Thursday, January 20, 1972
One Day Before the Game

It took 16 speakers to do the job. Mr. Barrett trimmed the speaker boxes in maple to match the gym floor. Two senior boys got a nice two-day break from classes to sand and stain the pieces.

Mr. Turner sent a wiry seventh grade boy into the ceiling crawl space with a flashlight and a coil of speaker wire. He especially yearned to install speakers in the bathrooms. The acoustics there were fabulous. The sound reverberated between the rounded corners of the plaster walls.

The sound was so realistic that Junior, walking past the gym late to class during the final sound check, rushed into the gym expecting to see a Nez Perce drumming group.

"Shee, Mr. Barrett, Mr. Turner, pull an old Indi'n trick on me, enit? It sounded like the real thing!" he laughed.

When Mr. Richardson heard the Rapid River Boys at full volume after school, he said, "Gentlemen, that's it! That's what I felt the first time I went to a pow-wow." The two long-time colleagues smiled and gave each other some skin.

25

Friday, January 21, 1972
Lapwai Wildcats Versus Latah Valley Falcons
Second Regular Season Game

Big Ron Harper just happened to enter the Lapwai High School gym entryway as a new song began over the sound system. The slow, steady drumbeat could've been the sound of a dozen basketballs striking the floor. But the JV's were not yet on the court. Big Ron wanted to get there early to get a good seat. He knew that the balcony back row seats provided poor views. He didn't know what to expect tonight.

After he stomped the snow from his work boots and took off his heavy plaid wool jacket in the toasty building, the drumbeat tempo increased, and the drummers began a low deep-toned chant.

"What the hell's this?" Big Ron grumbled to his wife Lorraine as he handed Mr. Richardson their tickets.

"It's a Grass Dance song," came a quiet voice a few feet from the gym entrance. An elderly man turned slightly in his front row seat and looked up at Big Ron. His upside down hat was half full of popcorn.

"The dancers are like sweet grass swaying in the wind," Josiah Whitehawk continued and then turned back around toward the empty court.

"Oh, well, uh, thank you," said a bewildered Big Ron.

"'Eehé."

Mr. Richardson smiled. That exchange was exactly what he was hoping for.

5:45 PM

When Lapwai's early arrivers heard the war-dance music over the new sound system, they could not stay still. For the Nez Perce, there was never a time before drums. They felt them as they felt their own heartbeats. It was in the cadence of their speech, in the rhythm of kneading dough for fry bread, and in the splitting of firewood to heat sweathouse rocks. Several elders danced in place waiting at the concession stand, an arm raised chest high, as if holding a ceremonial stone club, or a fan of eagle feathers.

Soon, the visitors from Latah Valley fell under the drum's spell. Chatter faded. They started to recognize the pattern of pow-wow songs...the gradual tempo increase, the occasional change from four notes-per-measure to two, the singers' call-and-response, and the way songs might abruptly end with a dramatic, final drum stroke. Now, throughout the gym, bodies kept beat with the drum.

Latah Valley did not know what to anticipate tonight: the sellout crowd, the advance-ticket sales, Lapwai's response to the first game's events... But they definitely did not expect this. They felt something new. They were beginning to get Lapwai.

6:00 PM

The JV's played in front of a crowd as big as this one once before. The previous year they played an afternoon game in Lewiston against the Sacajawea Junior High School ninth graders. Their entire student body attended. It was thrilling. The Sacajawea students (under the watchful eyes of their teachers) were courteous, and the Wildcats won a close, well-played game.

In fact, they also beat Jenifer, the other junior high school in Lewiston, that year. The game at Latah Valley stuck out as an ugly memory. Since then they were 10 and 0. Their confidence was back, and a large crowd was behind them. The pregame war dance music pumped them up even more.

Coach McNeese decided Terry needed more playing time than he'd probably get against the Latah Valley varsity, so Terry suited up with his classmates. With him running the show, it was a whole new ballgame.

Terry tied it with a fifteen foot bank-shot halfway through the third quarter. With a sold-out gym, the pep band had to stake out their seats early. Mr. Groves decided to fire up the JV's a little more. "School Song!" he shouted, and Jessica and her fellow musicians shuffled "The Notre Dame Fight Song" to the front of their quarter-sheet music holders.

A packed crowd. School Song playing for them. For the next twelve minutes, it was all Lapwai. The JV's avenged their loss in Latah Valley 60-51.

7:30 PM

Billy, Luke, and Junior watched the end of the JV game from the corridor doorway to the coaches' room. They high-fived each other as Terry took the game over and the JV's pulled away. This felt entirely different from the last Latah Valley game.

Coach McNeese brought the players together and explained the pre-game events. As the JV's came in, the boys stood in line at the locker room door and congratulated them. "Your turn," Terry urged his varsity teammates.

To a thunderous ovation, the varsity ran toward mid-court. Halfway, they slowed to a near stop, just as Justin Murphy casually flicked the ball over the front of the rim at the other end. The boys had read about the Portland transfer's points in the Lewiston Morning Tribune sports section. It never mentioned six foot six.

7:50 PM

Reverend Matthews stepped onto the court in front of the scorers' bench as the two squads finished warm-ups. He raised the microphone and in a clear voice addressed the silent crowd in Nez Perce. To Sam, the sounds always made him think of river water in forest canyons.

Reverend Matthews saw perplexed expressions, but also many content smiles. Several elders nodded in agreement as he welcomed the guests from Latah Valley. In English, the message became clear. "We're glad you're here... Play ball!" Reverend Matthews handed the microphone to Mr. Richardson.

"Tonight we'd like everyone to help us honor one of the best fans in north central Idaho," said Mr. Richardson. "We discovered that Mr. Whitehawk has only missed three home games in 42 years. Three sons and seven grandsons played for the Wildcats. He is in the same front row seat for every JV tip-off. For his faithful support, we would like to present Josiah Whitehawk with a lifetime pass to all Lapwai High School events."

Mr. Whitehawk slowly stood. He handed his hat, full of popcorn, to Sam's mother sitting beside him. He shuffled toward Mr. Richardson at center court and took the microphone.

"Thank you for this honor. I want to say that it has brought me great happiness over the years to watch the boys play basketball. I wish both teams good luck tonight. I will always remember this night and look forward to many more seasons. But I may need a ride sometime soon. My kids tell me I'm turning into a bad driver." The crowd laughed appreciatively. "Again, qe'ciyéw'yew'."

Mr. Whitehawk then surprised everyone by turning toward the Latah Valley bench. He lightly shook Coach Bradley's hand. "That one-three-one of yours is one tough defense."

"Thank you, sir," replied an amused Roy Bradley. Josiah Whitehawk waved to the cheering crowd. He was relishing the moment. Mr. Richardson accompanied Josiah Whitehawk back to his seat.

Nez Perce Veterans Honor Guard

Mr. Richardson returned to the scorers' bench. "Ladies and gentlemen, please stand for the presentation of the flags of the State of Idaho and of the United States of America." The lights dimmed. The only sound was the faint cadence of the Nez Perce Veterans Honor Guard, marching two abreast. "Left, left, left, right, left..."

The four veterans represented the four wars of the twentieth century. The youngest, Melvin Highmoon, carrying a parade rifle in the second row, returned from Vietnam three years earlier. Beside him, his older cousin Herman limped slightly from a North Korean bullet. He bore his Purple Heart on a leather vest beaded with an image of an unfurled American flag. The third member, James Redheart, carrying the Idaho state flag, saw action in North Africa during World War II.

The honor of carrying the American flag was bestowed on the oldest armed forces veteran of the Nez Perce Tribe of Idaho. Harold Moffett was 27 years old when he enlisted in 1919. The 80-year-old elder set a slow but steady pace.

They neared the flag stands at the southeastern corner of the gym stage. James commanded, "Honor guard, halt," and then, "Honor guard, post the colors." Mr. Moffett and Mr. Redheart positioned their flags. As one, the honor guard stepped backward and raised their right hands to their military caps in salute.

A drum roll from the Lapwai High School pep band began "The Star Spangled Banner." The few remaining baseball caps in the crowd were snatched off. Voices throughout the gym were heard singing the national anthem.

Latah Valley and Lapwai folks shared this moment. The nation was at war. Watching Mr. Moffett saluting the flag, his chin thrust forward, standing tall, the crowd thought of their own boys serving their country halfway around the world and wished they were home watching their high school team play basketball.

No pow-wow drums, no fancy speeches, no war heroes could help Lapwai stop Justin Murphy's jump-hook. By now he was accurate out to eight feet from the basket. Either hand.

When Mike started 'fronting' Justin, Justin pivoted to the basket, caught Ron's lob, and scored. Two hours every Sunday Nick came over and they practiced more moves. Big Ron gave him $7.50 an hour for his time, twice what he got at the Grange.

When Coach McNeese tried a two-one-two zone, Ron Harper torched the Wildcats from outside.

As Latah Valley pulled ahead, Coach McNeese stuck with what he knew best- a ball control, slow tempo game. It didn't work. The starters stayed on the floor, exhausted and frustrated, while Sam and the rest of the second string watched from the bench. Latah Valley won by 16. The 'Cats shook hands with the Latah Valley players and retreated to their locker room.

Once inside, Coach McNeese consoled his team. "Well, we didn't expect that. This loss is on me, boys. I should've scouted them better. I didn't know Harper's cousin was that good." Coach McNeese walked over to his son and put his hand on Mike's shoulder.

"That's a tough shot to stop, once he turns to the basket. We got some things to work on. We're not done yet. Hands in the middle."

The boys huddled around Coach McNeese. "On three, 'Pride'," Billy, their team captain, said. They placed their hands on top of each other's, raised them together, and shouted, "Pride!"

Mr. Richardson stood just outside the locker door. "This was an amazing night," he thought. "And I have a feeling the boys'll bounce back from this one."

26

Mike finally got up the nerve, and Julia said "Yes." They double-dated with Vicky and Sonny, and after the Winter Dance they all went to Lewiston for dinner at the Red Shield.

As Mike entered the restaurant, he thought he recognized the couple in a nearby booth. Just as he was about to walk over and say "Hi," Vicky said, "Julia and I are going to the bathroom for a sec. Maybe you guys can find a table."

"Okay," Sonny answered. "We'll look over by the windows. You'll find us." Vicky and Sonny knew how to do this. They'd been going out for a while.

Sonny soon spotted an empty booth, and Mike and he sat opposite each other. Mike could see the familiar pair in the large mirror at the entrance. "Oh!" He remembered how he knew the couple. They were old college friends of his parents. They'd been to the house several times. Bud and Lois.

Mike caught Bud's eye in the mirror, and they both waved. Mike could see Bud lay his hand on his wife's arm and say something. Mike watched her smile and nod. But as they started to rise, their eyes traveled from Mike to Sonny sitting across from him. They froze. Just then Vicky and Julia walked past their booth, and when Vicky slid into the booth next to Sonny, and Julia sat by Mike, Mike watched his parents' old friends hurry to the cashier, retrieve their bill, pay, and rush out the door.

Mike stared out the window as Bud and Lois drove away. Then he remembered some of Bud's jokes after a couple of beers at backyard barbecues, and the way Lois cackled along with him. Mike's companions' voices sounded distant, as if they were coming from another world. He shook his head, turned toward his friends, smiled, and soon joined in their stories.

27

Sunday, January 23, 1972

Latah Valley's victory in The Rematch got three lines in the Boise Statesman sports section. They moved into first place in the state polls. Lapwai dropped to seventh.

January 24, 1972
3:15 AM

Coach McNeese couldn't sleep. He didn't want to admit it, but Mike couldn't handle Justin Murphy by himself. He recalled his own words. "That's a tough shot to stop, once he turns to the basket."

"We're going taller on Monday," Coach McNeese concluded, and at last fell asleep.

3:30 PM

That afternoon, Sam was a starter for the first time since JV's.

Coach McNeese broke down the mechanics of their new defense for the boys: a sagging man-to-man. "Sam, as soon as Harper passes inside, you and Mike double-team Murphy. Don't let him take that first step. Get those long arms up."

"Denny, I guarantee you are the best A-3 sixth man in the state. I'm sending you in at any position on the floor."

"Boys, I should have stuck with playing everybody. You're all players. We take District as a team."

Coach McNeese was as fired up as the boys had seen him. They were eager to tear through the last six regular-season games. At District, number one Latah Valley would be in one bracket, number two Lapwai in the other. They would probably meet again for the league championship. The Wildcats couldn't wait.

28

The Wildcats dominated the end of the regular season. Coach McNeese recovered his groove. "Shoot," he laughed to himself, "I've forgotten more basketball than most people ever know."

The boys quickly caught on to their new sagging man-to-man defense. It was stifling. Against Clearwater, they trapped the ball handler over and over. 19 turnovers. 27 points. Total.

Denny loved his new role. Together Coach McNeese and he watched for opposing defenses' weaknesses. Then Coach sent Denny in to do what he did best: shoot. "Being Sixth Man is way better than starting," Denny thought.

Everybody was playing lots of minutes again. District? Bring it on.

29

February 4, 1972

And Sam and Jessica? Well, with Sam starting, Jessica could watch him play more. She liked his passion for basketball. She saw genuine friendship between Sam and his Indian teammates. Jessica was falling in like with Sam.

Jessica's mother Ida also scrutinized the tall white boy who was interested in her daughter. She approved of what she saw. "This sooyáapoo is alright," she thought. "He comes from a good family. But Jessica still has to be home by eleven."

So Sam and Jessica had their first solo date. Sam was ready with a new list from Vicky called "What to Talk About with Jessica."

They followed Sonny and Vicky to Ervono's in Sam's old green pickup everyone called Norman Green Bomb after the final home game and talked. They talked about favorite movies (Jessica liked *Billy Jack*); colleges (Jessica wanted to go to Northern Arizona University); songs ("Band of Gold"); seasons (summer), and so on. Luckily, by the time they reached Lewiston Sam ran out of questions. Jessica was exhausted.

Sam got five more questions from Vicky at Ervono's while Jessica was in the bathroom, just in case. They shared a medium combination pizza, played some foosball, and soon it was twenty minutes to eleven.

"We better go," said Sam.

As they got in the pickup, Jessica wondered if she was going to have to answer more questions. Maybe they could do something else. "Do you have any music?" Jessica asked as she noticed the eight-track player under the dashboard.

"Sure. There are some tapes under the seat." Jessica slid toward the middle of the cab and reached down. She pulled out a wooden box holding 24 tapes and picked out a collection of Top 40 hits called "Rock 28."

"How's this?"

"That's a good one," Sam answered. Jessica pushed the box back under the seat, inserted the tape, and squeezed a matchbook from the tape box under the eight-track to keep it from jiggling. She decided to stay where she was.

They listened to "Peace Train" by Cat Stevens, and Jessica remembered the last time they rode home together. It was nice. Jessica reached over and took Sam's hand. They traveled home quietly that way. It was how they both preferred it.

As they crossed Spalding Bridge, Sam noticed the reflection from the last ice floes of the season backed behind the bridge piers. Ice was finally breaking up in the dark, narrow canyon between Orofino and Kamiah. A full moon rose overhead.

"Look!" Sam pointed toward the park. Three deer stood among the trees in a beam of moonlight. Just below them, the mill trace was hidden in darkness. Sam suddenly felt Jessica's hand go cold.

"What's wrong?" he asked, alarmed. Sam turned to see Jessica's ashen face in the dark pickup cab. They were well past Spalding before she spoke.

Finally, she said, "I just got this really weird feeling. I just felt, I don't know, really sad."

"Long Shadow..."

"Definitely. I'm okay now." Jessica squeezed Sam's hand. They drove away from the place Aunt Milly's best friend May lost her brother's knife so many years ago.

"I don't know what happened," Jessica repeated.

"Chize...I don't know what happened, either."

"But I *do* know," thought Sam. "Should I tell her?"

30

February 13, 1972

"What's happening to me?" Jessica needed help. She needed someone who knew the old ways. Suddenly she remembered the kind elder who taught the girls traditional dances at the Pi-Nee-Waus.

Aunt Milly again awaited her young visitor. She had a piece of pie already sliced for Jessica when the knock came on the door. Aunt Milly's smile told Jessica she wouldn't have to explain her late afternoon visit. *"Ta'c halá p[11]*, Auntie," Jessica simply said.

"I am so glad that you knew you could come to me," Aunt Milly replied. "Come in."

Jessica glanced at an open photo album in the next room. "Do you want to see a picture?" Aunt Milly asked. Jessica nodded. They passed through the archway into the dining room. Aunt Milly turned the group photograph of the children hospitalized at the Fort Lapwai Tuberculosis

---

[11] täts\hə\LAUP

Sanatorium Jessica's way. Jessica stared at the slender girl with waist-length hair in the back row who wore her face.

Jessica whispered, "What does this mean, Auntie?"

"Do you want to know her name?" Jessica nodded. "It's May. She was my best friend." A chill ran through Jessica, and she grasped the back of a wooden dining chair.

"Let's sit down," Aunt Milly suggested. Jessica gratefully sank into the comfort of the old couch. Her left hand played with the fringe of a flowered shawl draped over the couch arm. The tick-tock of the fireplace mantel clock helped calm Jessica's racing heart. Aunt Milly waited until she saw Jessica was ready.

"May has something very powerful for you. It is very special to be chosen for this, Jessica." Aunt Milly looked into Jessica's eyes and continued.

"Sam told me what happened sledding and in Lewiston that night." Aunt Milly paused. "The boys were saved by a special power. May wants to pass it on to you. It's the power of her guardian spirit." Jessica's eyes froze on Aunt Milly's soft face.

"After Sammy left, I thought a long time about May. How she watched out for the other children at the hospital. There was this one time a little girl took a mirror from the doctor's table. They found it under her clothes. She was going to get in big trouble. Instead, May took the blame. She had to stay in a little room all by herself, hardly any food.

Two days. I asked her about it. She just said, 'It's my duty'."

A tear trickled down Jessica's cheek. She tried to imagine how it must have felt to do that for another person. Jessica wanted that kind of courage.

"May is not at rest here, Jessica. I don't know why yet, but I will. She sees the same quiet strength in you she had."

"I don't feel strong."

"Do you love your family?"

"Yes. Of course."

"Do you love your friends?" Jessica nodded.

"Love is your strength," Aunt Milly explained. "It grows every day."

Jessica thought about the people she cared about and remembered May.

"What is my power, Auntie?"

"It's not yours yet, *Sayáq'ic húukux*[12]."

Pretty Hair. Jessica was surprised Aunt Milly knew her Indian name honoring an ancestor who went away over a hundred years ago.

Aunt Milly explained. "You must be prepared first to receive it... It's the power to *protect*."

"Can you teach me, Auntie?"

"I was hoping you'd ask. Yes, of course." Then she added, "I have no choice."

Jessica nodded. She was beginning to see the special power of Aunt Milly's guardian spirit.

---

[12] so\YÄKH\its\hü\huk

"Remember," Aunt Milly warned, "this must be kept inside you, Jessica. You cannot share this with anyone else or the power will be diminished." Aunt Milly smiled. "Now... Do you want some pie?"

Moments later, Aunt Milly returned from the kitchen with a warm piece of apple pie, handed it to Jessica, and dropped into her chair next to the couch. "There's something else I need to tell you," she said. So while Jessica slowly ate her pie, Aunt Milly retraced the passage of the small, white pocket knife from May's brother to May, to Aunt Milly, to Sam, to May again, and back to Sam.

"May always believed she and the knife belonged with her brother. I believe you have a special part in bringing them together again, Jessica."

Just then they heard footsteps outside. Through the narrow glass door-pane Aunt Milly saw the blue and white outline of a Lapwai High School letterman's jacket. She slowly rose and crossed the room to the front door.

"Sammy, come in! We were just talking about you," Aunt Milly said as they hugged.

"Ta'c halá p, Redwing," laughed Jessica. A delicate china dessert plate sat on the couch cushion beside her.

"Apple. My favorite," Jessica explained. "But coconut cream is good, too." Coconut cream just happened to be Sam's favorite.

Sam felt like he had just walked in halfway through a movie. Then he remembered that Aunt Milly helped Jessica learn pow-wow dances at the Pi-Nee-Waus. They'd become friends.

"Good afternoon to you, She-Who-Shows-Up-in-Surprising-Places," Sam replied. Jessica laughed.

"Jessica saw your picture on the TV over there, and she said you two are friends." Aunt Milly suddenly grew somber.

"Jessica knows about the knife now, Redwing. She's going to help."

Jessica nodded. No one spoke. The ticking of the old clock echoed in the background.

"Do you want some pie?" Aunt Milly finally asked Sam.

"Of course, Auntie. Qe'ciyéw'yew'." Sam took the empty couch seat.

"This is all so cool," thought Jessica.

"Do you come see Aunt Milly a lot?" Jessica wondered.

"Did you know we used to live next door? I played with her nephew Gordy in the summer." Sam stood, walked to the television console, and held up Gordy's graduation picture. "He lives in Oregon now."

Aunt Milly handed Sam his pie and sat down. They discussed many things. Aunt Milly told stories about week-long spring camas root harvests. When the talk turned to the district tournament starting the following week, Sam reiterated that his mother would be glad to give Aunt Milly a ride.

"I'd really like to go. Tell her thanks, Sammy."

"Okay. Well, I better take off."

Sam didn't need to ask Aunt Milly what to do now. She already took care of it. And it couldn't be better. Somehow Jessica and he would return the knife to May's brother.

"Come over Saturday morning. I'm showing Jessica how I make fry bread," said Aunt Milly. Her eyes sparkled.

"One more thing, Sammy. When you shoot free throws, don't forget to bend your knees."

"Thanks, Auntie. I will." He laughed to himself. "Great. Now everybody in Lapwai thinks they're basketball coaches."

31

Sam bent his knees, raised his shooting arm to a 90 degree angle, steadied the ball with his left hand, and with his fingertips curved, propelled the ball with just his wrist. His right hand arced straight toward the center of the net. Swish.

Sam imagined the crowd's roar. He looked up at the empty balcony where Jessica would be sitting in the clarinet section.

"Might as well shoot around. I could be here a while waiting for those two girls."

The league's high schools' principals rotated serving as the district basketball tournament director. It just so happened it was Mr. Richardson's turn. At that moment, he was in Lewiston finalizing the program at the printers.

Sam was the Lapwai High School student body president. Julia was vice-president. Traditionally, the ASB president and vice-president helped with last-minute chores at Lewiston High School's Booth Hall. That morning Mr. Richardson had stashed long paper banners the fourth-year art class painted bearing the league members' names in the back of his station wagon. Sam and Julia's first job was to hang them where the towns sat for their first two games.

A day earlier, Sam and Julia stood outside the principal's office. As always, at Julia's side was Vicky.

"Mr. Richardson, Sam and Julia can't put up the signs by themselves. Two people have to hold the ends, while someone else puts on the tape. Besides, it wouldn't look right for Sam and Julia to go by themselves."

Mr. Richardson smiled. He was used to being talked into things by Vicky. He thought to himself, "She's a great kid. She can miss a few classes."

So Sam, Julia, and Vicky headed to town in Norman Green Bomb. It was the perfect time to tell Vicky the latest on May's knife. Sam and Vicky would be careful what they said around Julia.

But Julia didn't bat an eye as Sam recounted Aunt Milly's revelation, Jessica's eeriness at Spalding Park, and her wish to help return the knife to May's brother.

"So she held your hand?! Cool!" Vicky teased and elbowed Sam in the side.

"Yeah, it was nice. But what are we going to do about the knife?"

"You mean 'we' as in you and Jessica, or 'we' as in you, Jessica, and me? 'Cause admit it... You can't do this without my brilliant detective mind."

"Okay. I know you're right. You always are. So the three of us..."

"The four of us," interrupted Julia. Sam and Vicky turned in surprise to see Julia staring out the window, lost in thought.

"You guys can't know what this feels like for Jessica. I do. Jessica and I owe this to our elders." Sam and Vicky nodded in agreement. Julia slipped her left hand into Vicky's right. Vicky reached for Sam's hand.

"We'll find a way," whispered Julia.

32

Mr. Richardson was waiting for them outside Booth Hall as they parked.

"Is everything okay?" he asked, as Sam, Julia, and Vicky wordlessly ascended the front steps. Back at school he usually had to step out in the hall to hush the two girls. "Talk about energy! I need some of that," he often thought.

"Oh, we're fine," Vicky answered. "We were just talking about different stuff."

"Oh...okay." Mr. Richardson couldn't imagine them staying this quiet for long. "Anyway, the signs are on the bottom rows where they go up. There's tape by the door. You'll see when you go in. After you guys get done, I'll be in the foyer and I can give you the next job."

"Okay, Mr. Richardson," they answered together.

It took about an hour to put up the eight signs. Vicky made them redo the first three signs because she thought they were crooked. After they finished the last one, Vicky realized the signs were all too low.

"What if a whole bunch of big farmers sat on the top row and they all had cowboy hats on? You wouldn't be able to see the signs." Sam and Julia looked at each other and sighed.

"If a row of farmers were already sitting in the bleachers, everyone from that town would recognize them, and they would know that was where they were supposed to sit," Sam thought. But Sam and Julia both knew better than to argue with Vicky. They raised each sign as high as the girls could reach.

"There!" Vicky declared. They admired their work from center court. Bold letters stood out in each school's colors. On one side of the gym, the banners read: Potlatch; Kamiah; Prairie; Kendrick. Opposite them were their first game opponents: Clearwater; Timberline; Latah Valley; Lapwai.

Latah Valley? Lapwai? Next to each other? As the three teenagers inspected the banners, Mr. Richardson approached them with a pleased expression.

"Did he do that on purpose?" Sam wondered.

They helped Mr. Richardson put up signs directing fans to the restrooms and concessions. Soon it was time for the students to get back to school. Sam had practice in 45 minutes.

"We'll just be a sec, Counts," Vicky said. The girls headed to the restroom. Sam stepped back into the dark and empty gym. Exit sign lights lit the gym with the reddish glow of a sunset. Sam could barely decipher the nearest banner. *Lapwai.*

Sam pictured the scene in two days. Timberline and Kamiah are in the third quarter. The team steps off the bus and enters the gym. Lapwai fans already fill most of Booth Hall's south bleachers. Mr. Groves summons the band to play the school song. As the band finishes, Junior stops and hollers what someone always shouts whenever a group of Lapwai people sit together.

"Where's the Indi'n Section?" A roar of laughter answers him.

The Indi'n Section... On the lower rows, older Nez Perce wear windbreakers bearing the names of all-Indian basketball tournaments from across the West. Toppenish. St. Ignatius. Wind River. Next to them sit their white neighbors who farm the hilltops and gulches surrounding narrow Lapwai Valley. On the top rows the high school kids, Indian and white, hang out. They talk and laugh. Always the laughter, in unison, unlike a sound heard anywhere else, one Sam would never forget. Sam loved sitting in the Indi'n Section.

The Indi'n Section would be out in full force Thursday night for the Wildcat's tournament opener against Kendrick.

Central Idaho League

33

Central Idaho League District Tournament
Opening Round
Lapwai Wildcats Versus Kendrick Tigers
February 17, 1972

Kendrick sits in a picturesque side canyon off the Clearwater 17 miles from Lapwai. Locust trees flourish in the summer heat captured in the narrow gorge. In late spring, their blossoms fill the air with sweet fragrance.

In early spring, though, Potlatch Creek roars down the canyon with mountain-snow runoff. Pioneers were smart enough to build their town above the flood line, but low-lying alfalfa fields receive frequent drenchings.

Witty sportswriters might have written headlines like "Lapwai Soaks Kendrick" or Kendrick Gives Way Under Lapwai Torrent." The Lewiston Morning Tribune simply stated "Kendrick Loses to Lapwai 74-46 at District."

Terry was high-point man against Kendrick with 16, and Sam had a season best 12 points. It was a good start for District. The 'bench' played a lot, so the starters were fresh for Kamiah.

After the boys got on the bus to go eat, Coach McNeese congratulated the team. "Good game! We stayed with what we do and didn't get sloppy." Then he grinned. "Practice at 8:30 tomorrow."

"Practice tomorrow?!" the team reacted in surprise.

"Yep. Short one. You're excused from first period. You remember the top two teams go to State this year?" The boys nodded. "We get past Kamiah, we're there."

With six A-3 leagues across the state and an eight-team tournament, every three years the Central Idaho League sent two representatives. 1972 was one of those years.

Coach McNeese continued. "While you boys are stuffing your faces with spaghetti and fried chicken, I'll be watching our next opponent. See you in the morning. Good game." Coach McNeese stepped off the bus and walked back in the gym.

Coach McNeese knew something the boys didn't. Three times in the last 12 years Kamiah finished the regular season in the middle of the pack only to end up surprising people at District and going to State. "Not this year," Coach McNeese promised himself.

Kamiah and Prairie were already halfway through the first quarter when Coach McNeese found a seat five rows above the scorers' bench. He loved this part of his job, seeing his peers' styles and strategies. Fred Spencer was one of the best. "Okay Fred, let's see what you got up your sleeve."

Kamiah led by three. Prairie brought the ball up court and set their offense. As the Pirates worked the ball around, Coach McNeese spotted something familiar: when the ball went inside, the post player was quickly double-teamed. If he was lucky, he got it back to his point guard. Otherwise, turnover.

"Sagging man-to-man," chuckled Coach McNeese. "Thanks, Fred. We've been seeing this in practice the last three weeks. Now...what about offense?"

A Prairie Pirate forced up a 15-foot jumper, and Kamiah's six foot one center chased down the rebound. Kamiah slowly brought the ball up the court. Coach McNeese instantly understood what was going on.

"They're not very tall, and Fred doesn't have the athletes this year. He's slowing the game down." The Kubs took 45 seconds off the clock until their umpteenth pass found a wide-open player just inside the foul line. He sank a routine jump shot that gave Kamiah a five point lead.

And so on. Kamiah controlled the tempo, frustrating Prairie's young coach to no end. Final score: Kamiah 35, Prairie 26.

34

Lapwai Wildcats Versus Kamiah Kubs
February 17, 1972

"Kamiah wants to slow things down," explained Coach McNeese the next morning at mid-court. The boys groaned.

"I know. You want to run."

They smiled. "You got us figured out, Coach," laughed Billy.

Ray McNeese continued. "So we're going to speed things up. It's something new for us, but I think you'll like it. It's called a half-court trap."

For the next 45 minutes the first and second strings took turns practicing the fundamentals of the half-court trap. Coach was right. The guards loved attacking the ball. They knew, come game time, they could go all-out. Fresh teammates were ready to step in.

Kamiah was no match for Lapwai's depth. The half-court trap worked perfectly. When the 'Cats didn't force a turnover out front, Mike, Sam, Denny, Luke, and Junior picked off desperation passes underneath. The rattled Kubs abandoned their sagging man-to-man, and Sonny and Billy found Mike and Sam in the paint over and over.

When the 'Cats led by 18 midway through the third quarter, Coach McNeese turned it over to the second string. The starters watched the rest of the game from the bench, resting for Saturday night's championship. Final score: 65 to 46.

35

While Latah Valley was taking care of business in the other bracket, a completely different story was playing out in the south bleachers where Lapwai and Latah Valley fans sat.

Most folks attending the Central Idaho League District Tournament left after their teams played. They dined at one of Lewiston's many fine restaurants before making the long drive back home in the country.

Not Lapwai. They were there for the long run. There was nothing they'd rather do more than watch high school basketball. Besides, Lapwai, 12 miles away, was by far the closest Central Idaho League town to Lewiston.

So Lapwai and Latah Valley fans watched the Falcons' first two district games side-by-side. They squeezed in to make room for latecomers. They smiled at their toddlers playing together along the sidelines by the bottom bleacher row. They cheered the fine play of Latah Valley's excellent team. As any passionate fan will tell you, "Good basketball's good basketball, whoever's playing."

Many Latah Valley folks were hearing, <u>really</u> hearing, Indians for the first time. "They're so funny!" Soon, Lapwai and Latah Valley folks were visiting. Hunting. Fishing. Crops. The weather. Basketball.

Sam's mother Carol drove both Aunt Milly and Josiah Whitehawk to the Wildcats' first two games. Aunt Milly and she patiently watched the very end of each night's games while Mr. Whitehawk scrutinized each contest with a master's eye.

Between the Lapwai-Kamiah game and Latah Valley's clash with Clearwater two familiar faces found seats next to Carol, Aunt Milly, and Mr. Whitehawk.

"Good to see you again," Josiah Whitehawk said as he turned toward Big Ron Harper and his wife Lorraine. "We spoke at the big game down to Lapwai couple weeks ago." Mr. Whitehawk took Big Ron's hand in a soft embrace. "You really took it to us that night. Your nephew had a really good game."

A pleasantly surprised Big Ron responded, "Thank you. We were all happy with how that game turned out for us. Your Lapwai boys have a solid team."

"They're coming along pretty good," agreed Mr. Whitehawk. "Your son, he's real solid himself. He plays like an Indian..."

Big Ron froze. "Now just a minute..." Beside him, Lorraine felt her stubborn husband tense and patted his hand. She leaned in front of Big Ron and turned toward the Nez Perce elder she recognized from the unforgettable pre-game ceremonies three weeks earlier.

"Thank you very much, Mr. Whitehawk. We're very proud of our son."

Josiah Whitehawk continued. "...He plays like an Indian I saw 16, 17 years ago. A Crow name of Gilbert Yellowtail. Went on and played for Montana State. Heard of him?" The Harpers politely shook their heads. "Played a lot like your son does. Good shooter, saw the whole floor...don't know how he got that ball in there on some of those passes. Best Plains Indian I ever saw play. Run all day. Nowhere to hide out there on the prairie, I guess. You got to be fast, or you get shot." Mr. Whitehawk quietly chuckled to himself, nodding his head up and down.

Big Ron relaxed. "Thank you, sir. That means a lot to us. I can see you're a big basketball fan."

"I watch as much as I can. Getting harder to get around nowadays," Josiah Whitehawk admitted. "I saw your son was going to be real good couple years ago on the JV's. I always wondered, though, when somebody was going to finish teaching him how to go to the hoop."

Big Ron was curious. "There's something my son could learn about driving to the basket? I always thought that was one of his strengths."

Josiah was in his element. He was talking basketball, and he had Big Ron right where he wanted him. He made the most of it.

"Oh, he can blast past about anybody. He's faster than any of these other boys in the league, except maybe our Jesse. He goes to Idaho next year, different story."

"How so?" Big Ron asked.

"Well, I can always tell which way he's going. He jab-steps all right, but he always goes the side he's dribbling."

Big Ron thought a moment. "The old man's right," he realized.

"If he worked on a cross-over dribble, it'd be harder to guess which way he's going. Fool 'em, enit?"

Big Ron made a mental note. He knew exactly what Mr. Whitehawk was saying.

"That's very good advice, Mr. Whitehawk. I'll work on that with Ron as soon as we have a chance. Thank you very much."

"Glad to be of service. This old Indian may not be able to lace up the sneakers anymore, but I learned a few things over the years." Josiah Whitehawk looked up. "Looks like they're ready to tip it off. I hope your son has a good game."

"Me, too," Big Ron replied. "And thanks, again."

Carol Evans smiled to herself. She had listened to the whole conversation. She looked toward the exit sign and saw that someone else was watching Josiah Whitehawk and Big Ron Harper talk. Carl Richardson and she caught each other's eyes and smiled.

36

If Sam and his friends could return the knife to May's brother, would she reach the Afterworld? Would she finally be with her ancestors, at peace?

Sam pondered the question. He remembered the night Vicky and he watched the shadows in Mrs. Preston's room, Room Five. "Lost souls," he lamented. Maybe they could help at least one of them.

Sam grabbed his "L" coat off the banister where he tossed it the night before. "Do you want me to go ask Aunt Milly what time she wants to go to Lewiston?" he shouted to his mother in the kitchen.

"That'd be great, Sammy. Thanks."

"Okay. Be back pretty soon." Sam jumped into Norman Green Bomb and headed to Aunt Milly's with Question Number Four.

37

"Redwing! Come in. Jessica and I are working on a new pair of pow-wow moccasins," Aunt Milly explained. A bowl of fry bread dough sat on the kitchen counter next to the oven. On the dining room table, Sam saw that a cluster of blue and white flowers was finished on one of the moccasins. School colors.

"Are you following me?" Jessica teased.

"Do you want me to?" laughed Sam.

Aunt Milly smiled at her two young friends. "There's plenty of pie for both of you."

Sam sat in the leather chair next to the fireplace. Grandpa's chair. A warm fire cut the mid-February morning chill. As Aunt Milly watched Sam stare into the flames, memories came flooding back.

"Jessica, let's stop for a while. Would you two like to hear a story?"

Aunt Milly knew why Sam was here.

"Of course, Auntie," they answered together.

Aunt Milly sat in her favorite place, and Jessica brought one of the dining room chairs close to the fire. Sam stirred the embers and stoked the fire. Milly sipped from an old tin cup with blue flowers painted on it. Sam hadn't seen that cup since Milly told Gordy and him stories on rainy days.

Aunt Milly closed her eyes. Sam and Jessica waited. Soon, she looked up and held her open hands upward. Everyone was ready for some Indian storytelling.

Long ago, Coyote had a daughter. She was very pretty and kind, and a great comfort to Coyote in his old age. She took care of him, for Coyote was so ill with tuberculosis he hardly ever went out. She always had good things for him to eat, even in winter. Coyote did not want to lose her, but he knew she would marry soon.

Many suitors wooed her, but of all of them Otter was the most persistent. Coyote did not like Otter. Otter was not a very important person. He was very kind hearted, though, and made himself useful around Coyote's house. When the river froze he cut holes in the ice so Miss Coyote could get water. He also caught salmon for her to take to Coyote's cave. She and Otter both felt these kind acts would soften Coyote's heart toward Otter, but when Coyote saw the salmon he yelled, "Daughter, do not bother me with these winter salmon! They are no good. The only thing I want is venison soup."

"Oh, Father," she despaired, "how can I get venison at this time of year?" She rushed outside. Otter sympathetically offered to help, but there was nothing he could do. She ran away, neither knowing nor caring where she went.

Suddenly she stopped. There, alongside the trail, was the body of a partially eaten deer. A hind quarter was untouched, so she picked it up. "The Great Spirit intended this for my sick father," she rejoiced.

When Coyote saw the venison he exclaimed, "Daughter, I am grateful. This is just what I want."

Unfortunately, this deer was killed by five wolf brothers, and when they returned and found it missing, they followed Miss Coyote's trail. They were very angry and vowed to eat the thief. When they came to Coyote's house, the eldest wolf brother rapped loudly at the door. "Let us in! You stole our deer meat!"

Miss Coyote trembled. Coyote, though, knew the wolves didn't know who was inside. "Open the door, Daughter."

"I am afraid, Father," she cried, "with you so ill and I here alone."

"Nonsense," he answered. "They cannot harm us."

So she opened the door, and there stood five angry wolves, their fangs bared. But the wolves were pleasantly surprised, for they recognized Miss Coyote.

"Oh, sirs," she said shakily, "I am sorry I took your venison, but my father is very ill and I got it for him."

The eldest wolf brother exclaimed, "Coyote's daughter! We did not know it was you! Your father is a respected friend of ours, and we did not know he was ill. You are welcome to the meat."

Coyote overheard the conversation and called out, "Daughter, invite the wolves in so we may thank them."

So the wolves came in and visited at length with Coyote. All the while, the eldest wolf eyed Miss Coyote, and she glanced often at him. At last he said, "Coyote, I like your daughter very much. I ask your consent to try to win her."

Miss Coyote was filled with worry when her father repeated Wolf's words. "Daughter," Coyote explained, "you must marry soon, and Wolf comes *from a good family. I don't like that Otter one bit. He isn't your equal, and you will never be happy with him. Besides, I want a son-in-law who can take care of you and catch a deer once in a while. It is my wish you marry Wolf."*

She blushed but finally agreed, and she and Wolf were soon married by old Judge Porcupine. They built a new house near Coyote's. They lived happily together, and Coyote was content, too, for his daughter took care of both households. Besides, Coyote and Wolf were on the best of terms.

But their happiness was short-lived. Young Otter was grieved and jealous over the turn of events, and his whole family sided with him. They decided Otter must get revenge. So one dark night the Otters snuck up and set fire to the newlyweds' house. They burned to death.

As if on cue, their own dwindling fire burst back to life. Aunt Milly, Sam, and Jessica smiled and rocked their heads in unison. Aunt Milly continued.

"Ah ha!" exclaimed Otter as he hurried away. "You, Wolf, and you, Miss Coyote, you will cast me aside, will you?!"

Coyote was asleep in his own home during this horrible deed. In his dream he saw the souls of his daughter and her husband hasten over the mountains. Coyote shouted, "Daughter, don't leave me alone. Let me go with you."

She answered, "We are dead and you cannot come with us unless you, too, die. You must kill yourself."

Coyote asked, "How can I kill myself?"

"Any way you can," she answered. "Burn yourself up."

Coyote woke with a start. He rose and saw the smoldering ashes of his daughter's house and knew she was dead.

"My dream has come true," he said. "My daughter is dead. I will follow the vision, for I must go with her." So he set fire to his house and lay down in the flames. Soon, he lost consciousness and again saw his daughter.

"Daughter, I am coming," he shouted. "I did as you said."

She and Wolf waited for him on the crest of the Seven Devils Mountains. Together they journeyed on noiselessly, for they were spirits, you see.

But Coyote had not completely killed himself. He scorched himself so badly that his soul journeyed to the spirit land, but he was not entirely dead. As Wolf and his wife sped on farther and farther across the sky, Coyote fell behind. His soul had not entirely left Earth, and his daughter soon noticed.

"This will never do, Father," she said. "You will get no rest here. You must return to Earth."

"Very well, Daughter," said Coyote. "I will go back." He wept to leave her.

Aunt Milly stopped. "Redwing, would you go get some more wood?" Sam nodded and stepped out the back door to the shed.

Aunt Milly turned to Jessica and whispered, "What did Coyote have to do?"

"He had to let go." Aunt Milly nodded.

"And May?"

Jessica took her time to answer. "She has to let go, too."

"Let go of who, Sayáq'ic húukux?"

Jessica knew this one right away. "Her brother."

Aunt Milly smiled, placed her hand on Jessica's, and asked softly, "And...?"

Jessica looked at Aunt Milly quizzically.

"May has to also let go of her own life. The Earth life she never had," the elder explained. "She is keeping too much of her guardian spirit's special power for herself. It belongs here on Earth to protect the People. May belongs in the Afterworld now."

Aunt Milly brushed a lock of Jessica's long hair from in front of her eyes. "She will need a lot of courage. She will need your help."

Just then Sam walked back into the living room with an armload of firewood and laid three small locust tree limbs across the flames. Aunt Milly continued her story.

"I will make a small bundle for you. Pack this over the Five Mountains and you will again be an Earth dweller and never die. But never untie the bundle."

Coyote lifted the little pack and said, "Oh, this isn't heavy. I can run with this." He bade his daughter and Wolf farewell and started back for Earth. He climbed First Mountain with no trouble, and the second. At Third Mountain he tired, and the pack weighed heavily on his shoulders, but on he went.

But Fourth Mountain became terribly forbidding. He could hardly move one foot in front of the other. After much struggle he finally crossed it. Coming to the fifth and last mountain, he knew he could not carry his burden over its rugged crest. He finally said, "What's the use? I shall carry my load a little at a time."

Forgetting his daughter's warning, he untied the bundle and found nothing but old skeleton bones. He had been carrying them back to life from the land of death. Hurriedly, he crossed Fifth Mountain and at last re-entered the land of the living.

But he brought death with him in the skeleton bones, and from that day no one was truly happy, for all people now understood they must someday die. If Coyote had not untied the bundle before passing over Fifth Mountain, there would be no death in the world, and people would live forever.

For several moments the only sound came from the crackling fire. Finally, Sam broke the silence. "So May's burden is the knife? And after the knife is carried to her brother, she can cross the Five Mountains to the spirit land?" Aunt Milly nodded.

"Chize," was all Sam could say. Aunt Milly, Sam, and Jessica stared into the fire.

Then Sam remembered. "Oh! What time do you want to go to town? The first game starts at two."

"Let's go then. I don't want to just sit around here doin' nothin'."

"Okay. I better háamt'ic. I'll see you both at the game." Jessica gave Sam a warm smile.

"Remember, Redwing. Bend your knees for free throws. I'm watching."

Sam laughed and again said goodbye. "I can't wait to tell Vicky," he thought.

38

**Central Idaho League District Basketball
Championship Game
Lapwai Wildcats Versus Latah Valley Falcons
February 19, 1972**

Latah Valley coach Roy Bradley didn't scout any of Lapwai's remaining regular-season games. "I know what they're going to do. Run," he thought. He didn't see the Kendrick blowout, and Kamiah could never really run their offense. He hadn't seen Lapwai's sagging man-to-man defense.

Justin Murphy outstretched Mike for the opening tip-off. Ron Harper nabbed the ball and dribbled left-handed across mid-court. He jab-stepped right and then darted left. Only one thing was missing...the ball. He turned around in time to see Jesse lay it in.

Ron trotted down-court to bring the ball up. As they passed, Ron whispered, "Lucky." Jesse just smiled.

Ron glanced underneath at Justin, saw Sam in the passing lane, and dribbled toward the basket. This time, he jab-stepped left. Jesse sliced in front of him the moment he made his now predictable cross-over move to the basket. The Indi'n Section went wild.

After another easy lay-in, Jesse ran straight toward Ron. "Lucky? Again?" They brushed past each other as Ron angrily retrieved the basketball.

Jesse spotted a familiar sight on the bottom row. A ten-gallon hat full of popcorn sat on his lap. Josiah Whitehawk extended a clenched fist and Jesse gave the top of his hand a quick tap as he ran by.

This time Jesse grinned and asked Ron Harper, "One more time?" Instead, Ron hit Justin with a swift entry-pass.

Justin faked right, but as he pivoted, he turned into a waiting Sam. Justin lowered the ball. Instantly, Mike poked it loose. Sonny scooped it up and sped down the middle of the court. To his left, behind a back-pedaling Ron Harper, Billy angled toward the basket. Sonny pulled up and wrapped a pass around Ron to Billy mid-stride across the key. Less than a minute gone, and the Wildcats led by six.

"We just got to settle down," thought Coach Bradley. "Good move, McNeese, putting Waters on Ron. That boy's quick."

Now Jesse picked Ron up at the top of the Wildcats' key. He hounded Ron across the court. The referee counted out the seconds: "Six, seven..." Ron was completely flustered. With two seconds left to cross the mid-stripe, he pushed Jesse back with his left forearm.

The referee blew his whistle and placed his right hand behind his head. "Offensive foul! Number 12." Ron grabbed the ball with both hands and slammed it onto the gym floor. The whistle blew again.

"Technical, Number 12." Coach Bradley signaled the Falcon's junior point guard into the game. Ron stomped to the end of the bench.

Sonny sank both technical foul shots. With the technical, the Wildcats kept possession. Mike whipped the ball inbounds to Billy, who chucked it to Jesse at the top of the key. The Wildcats weren't letting Latah Valley set up their one-three-one zone this time. Two dribbles, and Jesse found Sonny open in the corner. Swish.

The 'Cats were on a 10-0 run against the number one team in the state. Now Coach Bradley called time-out. He had 55 seconds to keep this game from getting out of hand.

"We gotta hustle back on defense. Rusty, stay out front. Shot goes up, hurry back."

"They're dropping a player any time the ball goes inside. That means somebody's open. Justin, when you feel the double-team, pop it back out. They're in a sagging man-to-man. They're daring us to shoot outside. Let's show 'em. On three, 'Pass'...one, two, three..."

"Pass!" A composed Ron Harper squeezed into the huddle next to Rusty. "Let's go, man. Get us back in the game."

Rusty Bush dribbled the ball down-court. He glanced at the Falcon bench, and Coach Bradley gestured toward Justin. Rusty threw a chest-pass to Justin, who, in a flash, drew the double-team. He kicked the ball back to an open Falcon, who swung it back to Rusty on the right wing. He held the ball a moment, and just before the double-team arrived, tossed it back out front.

45 seconds ticked by. The Wildcats scrambled back-and-forth, unable to trap the ball-handler. Finally, Rusty found himself wide-open for an easy ten-foot bank shot. As soon as the ball rolled off his fingertips, Justin took off.

The Wildcats again pushed the ball up-court, but this time when Billy rose for a left-hand lay-in, he was met by six foot six Justin Murphy.

Thwack! Justin swatted Billy's shot against the backboard right to Rusty. Latah Valley fans popped to their feet. Rusty spotted a hustling Falcon down-court and whipped a two-hand overhead pass to him for a routine lay-in. Just like that, Latah Valley cut the lead to six.

For the rest of the first half Latah Valley controlled the tempo. With Ron Harper still on the bench with two fouls, the Falcons wore the Wildcat starters down with ball movement and that patient one-three-one zone defense.

Maybe if the Wildcats' early lead hadn't evaporated so quickly Coach McNeese would've stuck with his game plan. He had fresh players ready. Instead, the two teams ended up in a half-court duel. At halftime the Wildcats trailed by two.

"Well, Earl, old habits die hard."

"I let 'em play their game," Coach McNeese continued. "We need to run." Coach Guerreros nodded. They leaned against the training table in the coaches' room.

"What do you want me do, Ray?" Coach Guerreros ventured.

"Help me keep track of subbing. I get too caught up in the game."

"Alright!" Coach Guerreros thought to himself. "Everybody playing, these boys can run all day... Let's play some Indi'n ball."

Coach McNeese was ready to speak to his team now. He walked into the locker room and brought them together.

"We had them down once, we can do it again. Same starters." He paused. "But the Second Five checks in in three minutes." Coach Guerreros nodded.

"We're containing Murphy and took Harper out of his game, and we pushed it real well in the first quarter. And just five turnovers."

Coach McNeese continued. "We saw they can put five good ballplayers out there, but we got ten. We're gonna win or lose this one as a team." He paused. "Hey, get your heads up! We're going to State! Let's have some fun."

The boys put their hands together and shouted, "State!"

Back on the court, they heard it: "Let's go State! Let's go State! Let's go State!" The boys grinned. The dreams of a bunch of eight-year-olds come true. They were going to State. The pep band blared the school song, and the 'Cats circled the court before a few warm-up shots.

Again, Justin won the opening jump ball. This time, though, Jesse cut in front of Ron, picked-off the tip, and banked in a right-hand lay-in. 34 all. Brand-new ballgame.

Again, Ron passed to Murphy underneath. Instead of going inside-out, Justin pivoted into Sam's double-team. He dropped a two-hand pass over Sam to Ron in-stride for a lay-up, and the Falcons were back on top.

The Wildcats passed the ball in-bounds and looked for a quick score. The Falcons were already in their one-three-one defense. No fast breaks this half.

Sam, Mike, and Jesse circled the key while Billy and Sonny passed back-and-forth looking for an opening. Soon, Sonny found one. He hit Mike in the low-post. When Justin and Rusty Bush collapsed down, Mike found Sam free for a soft finger-roll.

The buzzer sounded and the second string rushed onto the floor. They were primed. They spent the first half watching Latah Valley's patient ball movement. With the Falcon guards staying back to stop the Wildcat fast break, Jimmy and Terry could take chances. When Ron lobbed a long, lazy pass to Rusty, Jimmy leapt and tapped it to

Terry. Ron cut off the sophomore guard at the top of the key. Terry slowed and crossed-over to his right. He flew past Ron standing flat-footed and laid it in. The starters went crazy on the bench. This time Ron kept his cool. His team needed him in the ballgame.

The lead swung back-and-forth. No team ever led by more than four points. When Coach McNeese played the Second Five, Coach Bradley rested his starters. Denny scored underneath with his smooth drop-step, and Luke got hot from 20 feet.

Bodies flew everywhere. Each player wanted the district championship, of course, but mostly they were having the time of their lives. Two great teams going all out.

With 25 seconds left and trailing by one, Coach McNeese called time-out. "Whatever happens, you played a heckuva game. I guarantee we play like this at State, we reach the championship. You ready?!"

Together all ten boys hollered, "Yes!"

"Let's do it!"

The crowd noise drowned out the referee's whistle as he handed the ball to Sonny. Sonny tossed it in to Billy. They again played catch on the wing, while the three interior players circled in the key. The clock ticked down to ten seconds. Latah Valley sagged back. The Wildcats would have to win it from outside. Five seconds. Sonny rose. As the ball left his fingertips, Sam could see it was off. The ball bounced off the front of the rim to Sam, and he tapped it back up.

All eyes followed the ball headed straight to the back of the rim. But just as it hit its peak, Justin Murphy managed to get a finger-tip on it. The ball careened sideways and fell into Rusty Bush's hands as time expired.

Latah Valley won the 1972 Central Idaho League District Championship 74-73.

Falcon fans poured onto the court. Coach McNeese frantically beckoned his team into a huddle.

"That was the best half of high school basketball I've ever seen!" he shouted. "I'm proud of you. Let's shake hands."

The teams met at mid-court. When Jesse and Ron passed each other, they smiled.

"Good game," Jesse said.

"You, too. See you at State."

"Count on it," Jesse promised.

The Wildcats turned toward the north-side bleachers and gave a familiar shout. "Where's the Indi'n Section?!" A huge cheer answered them. They donned their warm-up jackets, *Lapwai* emblazoned on the back, and headed to the showers and then back to the reservation.

Sunday, February 20, 1972

The Lewiston Morning Tribune sportswriters praised Lapwai's valiant effort the next day. Southern Idaho newspapers took notice. Latah

Valley stayed atop the A-3 state polls, but Lapwai trailed right behind at number two.

39

Sunday morning after District began sunny and warm. A soft wind carried hints of spring. The last patches of late winter snow melted in the shadows, and behind Sam's house the hillside was already turning green.

Sam considered his choices. Play basketball? Walk around town and see what happens?

He started for Luke's. As he rounded the corner, Sam heard the "Thunk!" of a bank shot against the backboard nailed to the front of Luke's garage. Without a word, Luke fed his friend cutting across the gravel. Sam laid it softly over the rim. They smiled and gave each other some skin. In three days they were going to State.

"What should we do?" Luke asked.

"Wanna go over to Jimmy's?"

Luke rolled the ball behind a leafless lilac bush, and they walked down the street. Jimmy sat on his front porch.

"What's happening?" he asked.

"Just walkin' around," Luke answered.

"Where to?"

"I don't know. We could go over to Sonny's."

Soon, the three boys found themselves at the Reuben's dining table getting advice while Sonny got dressed. A package of donuts was soon gobbled up.

"You guys need to shoot quicker. You're letting Latah Valley get back on defense," Sonny's mother scolded. Their mouths full, they politely nodded. Julia walked in and joined them at the table. Soon, Sonny was ready to go.

"We're just gonna walk around for a while," he explained to his mother, heading out the door.

Sam turned to Julia. "You wanna come?"

"Sure. Why not? We could go to Vicky's. Me and Vicky gotta talk about painting signs for State."

Soon, the group reached Denny and Vicky's house and added two more companions.

"Let's cut over to the creek," Luke suggested. "We can walk on the railroad tracks."

"Counts!" Vicky shouted. "You wanna go by Jessica's?" They stopped and turned toward Sam.

"Yeah. Why not? See if her mom lets her go." The group headed north toward Thunder Hill.

When Mrs. Whitehawk opened her front door, she almost shut it on the seven teens. Just in time, Sam asked, "Jessica here?" She stopped and looked from face to face.

"This is pretty much the Lapwai High School A Team," she thought. "These are good kids for my daughter to run around with."

"You wanna go?" She asked, as Jessica appeared behind her. Jessica smiled.

"I'll go get my coat," she answered. Moments later, she was walking beside Julia and Vicky on the train tracks back to Lapwai.

"Where you guys goin'?" Jessica asked.

"Oh, nowhere," Julia replied. "Just walking' around. See what happens."

Just then a magpie flew overhead. They could see its large, ramshackle nest near the top of a cottonwood tree beside the creek. In its mouth dangled a night crawler. Her chicks squawked for dinner.

"Hey," Jimmy said, "I heard if you cut a baby magpie's tongue, it can talk."

"In English or in Nez Perce?" Jessica asked. Everyone stopped and stared.

"No," Jimmy explained, "it talks in the language you teach it."

"Oh."

"So cute," Sam thought.

"So, you gonna do it?" Luke joked.

"I don't know. I'd like to look at them, anyway." They followed Jimmy through the bull thistles to the nest.

Jimmy clambered up the gnarled branches of the old tree. When he reached the magpie nest, he looked inside and then back to his friends.

"Anybody got a knife?" They stood, stunned. Would he really do it?

Sam reached into his pocket and pulled out a small, white Barlow knife. "This do?"

He felt a hand on his arm. He turned toward Jessica, pale as a ghost.

"Don't let him," she pleaded in a whisper. Sam held the knife. At that moment, Jimmy hopped to the ground.

"Psych! Had you guys goin', enit?! I wasn't going to do it. That'd be too weird. Anyway, I don't want no magpie."

They all sighed in relief. "So *yú'c*[13], enit?" Sonny broke the silence. "I almost believed you, man. I don't know about you Eastern Indi'ns." They all laughed. Everything was back to normal.

But as they started back to town, Jessica stood frozen in place. Sam turned and asked, "You all right?" He remembered her stricken look a moment ago. "You wanna go back?" She nodded. "I can walk back with you." Jessica gave Sam a quick smile.

"I'll catch up to you guys," he shouted ahead. Soon, Sam and Jessica heard their faint laughter behind them. Jessica knew she didn't have to explain anything to Sam.

"That was kinda scary for her," Sam thought. "She's not used to how we joke around. It'll be alright." They stopped at the end of the gravel path to Jessica's house.

"Thanks, Counts," Jessica said with a grateful smile. She reached out and squeezed his hand.

---

[13] yəts

"Anytime, She-Who-Protects. See you tomorrow in Band." He turned. Jessica watched Sam catch up to his friends and worried.

"Does he know?"

40

5:00 PM That Same Day

"Sayáq'ic húukux."

Halfway out the door, Jessica stopped and waved Julia on. "I'll catch you later," she called out. She walked back into the Gathering Room at the Pi-Nee-Waus and sat next to Aunt Milly.

They waited until the drummers finished stashing the pow-wow drum under a well-used pool table. On the drumhead the words *Nez Perce Nation Treaty of 1855* circled a silhouette of Chief Joseph. The same image adorned the Pi-Nee-Waus gym center court.

The drummers put on their coats, shook hands with Aunt Milly, and walked out laughing, the business end of their deerskin padded drumsticks sticking out the back pockets of their jeans.

Aunt Milly could finally ask: "What happened?" Jessica carefully recounted the magpie incident.

"When you thought Jimmy was going to cut the magpie chick's tongue, how did you feel?"

"I don't know, not scared exactly... When Sam took out the knife, I felt like someone was with me, guiding me, and I had to help those little birds."

Aunt Milly's face clouded.

"What is it?" Jessica gasped.

"You could have done that on your own," Aunt Milly explained. "May's time here must be over. She's already stayed too long. Now this... She cannot have your life."

Jessica shuddered. "What should I do?"

Aunt Milly laid a warm hand on Jessica's and closed her eyes. Jessica waited. Aunt Milly began singing, so quietly the sound seemed to come from far away. Jessica felt Aunt Milly sway back-and-forth, until her song faded into silence. She opened her eyes and spoke.

"The knife is a Power Object, Jessica. It attracted May's guardian spirit and helped her protect. But that power will be yours soon." Aunt Milly paused. "It's good Redwing holds the knife for now. This special power could weaken you until you are ready to help May let go of the knife."

Jessica looked into Aunt Milly's gentle eyes and whispered, "When will I be ready?"

Aunt Milly smiled. "You are on the right path, Sayáq'ic húukux, learning to follow our traditions. Someday you'll go on a vision quest. You will learn your own Power Song. It will help you call the strength of your guardian spirit. But May obstructs the path to your special power. You must trust your own strength. That is our way."

Oh! Jessica thought of Aunt Milly's song a few moments ago. She understood now what Aunt Milly risked by singing her power song aloud to help her learn.

Jessica knew she, too, would be called on to help her people. Would she have the strength to protect them on her own? Jessica thought of Sam and her other white friends. Who *were* her people?

41

Ida Whitehawk's pen hovered over the school trip form. "I give permission for my child _____ to participate in the State A-3 basketball tournament band trip to Boise, Idaho." Underneath read, "I can chaperone the Lapwai High School Pep Band at all tournament related activities. Signed, _____."

"Of course I want her to go to State," Ida thought. "But I just don't know about these kids nowadays. We never went out with boys when we were 15." In the back of her mind a thought took shape: "Especially white boys."

Ida Whitehawk had no reason to distrust the tall sooyáapoo her daughter liked. There were just so many responsibilities, with her husband Leroy still in Vietnam and three kids to look after. Thank goodness her family helped out. She glanced at Josiah Whitehawk in the next room, a blanket draped over his knees, absorbed in a college basketball game on TV. She smiled and walked to the living room doorway. Two birds with one stone.

"Uncle, you wanna go to State?"

42

Idaho A-3 State Basketball Tournament Opening Round
Lapwai Wildcats Versus Homevale Mustangs
February 24, 1972
6:00 PM

The first team in seven years from a reservation was going to State.

Two of the four Indian reservations in Idaho are in the Northern Panhandle- the Nez Perce and the Coeur d'Alene. A third, Fort Hall Reservation in the southeastern part of the state, is home to the Shoshone-Bannock tribe. The Duck Valley Indian Reservation overlaps a small part of the Idaho/Nevada border. Most small-school basketball players in southwestern Idaho might spend their entire careers without playing against an Indian.

Such was the case with Lapwai's first opponent, the Homevale Mustangs. They were ranch boys from the Snake River Breaks high desert. Die-hard cowboy country.

As people often do to those they don't know, Homevale folks made Lapwai into the 'bad guys.'

They sat in the Hitchin' Post Cafe on frosty mornings and swapped stories about Indians, which they shaped into truth. So the Mustang starting five begrudgingly shook hands with Sam, Mike, Jesse, Billy, and Sonny to open the 1972 Idaho A-3 Boys State Basketball Tournament.

Mike stepped into the center circle and looked at his Mustang opponent. What was it he saw? Anger? Contempt? As the referee started his jump-ball toss, the Homevale center sneered, "Let's get it on, Injun lover." Mike's feet never left the floor.

6:10 PM

Mike could do nothing right. He dropped an easy feed from Sonny. He threw a bounce pass straight to Billy's left foot. He clanked a lay-in off the bottom of the rim. So Homevale taunted him harder.

When a Mustang whispered something about 'tepee creeping,' Mike shoved him in the back. It was already his second dumb foul. Coach McNeese waved him over, and Mike collapsed next to his father.

Coach Guerreros got to work. But instead of Denny, Coach Guerreros sent Junior in for Mike. Coach McNeese raised his eyebrows. Junior could be, shall we say, 'somewhat of a loose cannon.' After the Mustang center sank both ends of the one-and-one, Homevale led nine zero.

"Watch," Coach Guerreros responded. "A little of their own medicine."

Just loud enough for the Mustangs to hear, Junior asked Sonny, "So, these cowboys wanna play Indi'n ball?"

Homevale's point guard dribbled down-court. But as Junior's man started across the key, he found his feet stuck in place. With his back to the referee, Junior clutched a handful of Mustang jersey. The pass rolled out of bounds.

"Old Indi'n trick," he laughed. "You sure you wanna play rez ball?"

"Go for it, Chief," snarled the irate Mustang.

Coach McNeese wasn't pleased. He liked a clean game. Then he glanced at his rattled son.

"People aren't very nice sometimes. Lapwai boys learn early how to survive," he realized. "They want to play dirty, I guess we can play that game, too."

When Coach Guerreros subbed Jimmy for Sam, all five Indian boys were on the floor together for the first time all season. This game wasn't about equal playing time. It wasn't about fresh legs. This game was about pride.

The boys started getting under Homevale's skin. They pestered their guards into turnovers slapping their dribbling hands. They stood on their rebounders' feet. They bumped their shooters' elbows just before their ball releases. They used every annoying trick passed down from cousins, uncles, and older brothers they knew.

Soon, the boys were shouting to each other in Nez Perce. After Junior harassed his man saying, "Só yú'c, 'aláamtit[14] sooyáapoo!" the Mustang player complained, "You gonna let him get away with that?!"

The referee laughed and shook his head. "*I* don't know what he said."

As the Wildcats crept back into the game, the Latah Valley folks awaiting the Falcons' upcoming clash got behind their northern Idaho neighbors. Homevale's ignorance was uncalled for. "Just play the game," grumbled Big Ron Harper.

Sonny tied the game at 24 with his soft 12-foot jumper. Jesse started down court but then spun around and picked off the careless in-bounds pass.

"Another old Indi'n trick," he laughed to a stunned Mustang.

Homevale's swagger dissolved, and the more talented Wildcats took over. At halftime, the Wildcats led by six.

The Indian boys started the second half and picked up where they left off. When the lead hit 14, Coach Guerreros sent in a fresh five.

Sam and his white teammates kept it going. When Sam went high to swat a Mustang lay-in halfway to mid-court, Denny yelled, "Don't bring that junior high crap in here!" Moments later, Terry juked the Mustang point guard in open court and laid in a sweet finger-roll. "Burned!" they shouted together. In the Wildcats' next possession, Luke jab-stepped right, pulled up, and swished a high arcing bomb. "In your face!" they laughed. When the

---

[14] ē\LƏM\tit

Wildcats led by eighteen they finally eased up. Final score: Lapwai 61, Homevale 47.

Mike watched his teammates fight this one together. "I get it now. This isn't about being white or Indian. This is about being from Lapwai." He thought about his teammates, Julia, and his other new friends. "I'm alright with being from Lapwai," he realized.

Coach McNeese huddled his team around him.

"You did what had to be done." He shook his head. "I learned something tonight...you don't mess with Lapwai." The boys grinned.

"Let's give 'em a yell... '*Náaqc*[15], *lepit*[16], *mitát*[17], Homevale'."

"You're turning into a real Indi'n, Coach!" Billy joked.

They raised their hands and shouted, "Náaqc, lepit, mitát, Homevale!" The Indi'n Section roared with laughter.

8:20 PM

Coach McNeese stood between the front seats of the Players' Bus.

"Enjoy dinner, boys. You earned it. I'll see you back at the rooms. I got some more work to do. Short practice tomorrow at nine."

---

[15] näks
[16] lä\PIT
[17] mē\TÄT

The boys smiled. 'Work'...right. Coach was an incurable basketball junkie. "Qe'ciyéw'yew', Coach," Billy said for the team.

Coach McNeese stepped off the bus and headed back to his favorite place in the world.

43

Travis Wheatley

The leading scorer in Idaho high school boys' basketball in 1972 wasn't a big man from, say, Boise, or a shooter from maybe Twin Falls or Nampa, or actually anyone from one of the big schools. He was a five foot eleven guard from Glenns Ferry, and he was the Wildcats' next opponent.

Travis Wheatley was a point machine. He could shoot from outside, score off penetration, and get to the foul line. His future already lay before him. Two years of junior college ball at Ricks College in Rexburg, serve his two-year church mission, and then on to Brigham Young University.

Coach McNeese had heard all about Travis Wheatley. "Quickest release you've ever seen." "Excellent off the dribble." "Great at using screens." Of course, Coach had to see for himself. Wheatley could do it all. Except pass.

8:25 PM

Coach McNeese bought two hot dogs and layered on some pickle relish. His hands full of basketball tournament dinner and a notepad in his coat pocket, Coach McNeese searched for a seat. He spotted an empty space on the front row next to an elderly Indian man eating popcorn from an upturned hat.

"Might as well," Coach McNeese thought. "Jeff's always telling me I need to be part of the community more."

"Excuse me...this spot taken?"

Josiah Whitehawk looked up. "Coach! Sit down! We'll talk some basketball." Coach McNeese took a seat.

"They told me I could stay for the next game and then call 'em later for a ride." The Nez Perce elder continued. "I see you got a couple of Indi'n steaks."

"You want one?" Coach McNeese enjoyed the way the Nez Perce often poked fun at themselves.

"Oh, no thanks, Coach. I got my popcorn. Too old to change my ways, enit?" Mr. Whitehawk chuckled. "Not like you, though. You been lettin' the boys run now."

"Well, sir, I guess you're right. Hard to hold 'em back."

"That's right. Been that way with us *titóoqans*[18] a long time. Us Indi'ns might even play some defense if we have to," Josiah Whitehawk chortled.

They quietly watched the Glenns Ferry Pilots warm up. Coach McNeese appreciated the Nez Perce elders' conversation pace. He didn't feel the need to always fill the air with noise, either. Finally, Josiah Whitehawk broke the silence.

"Yessir, Wheatley looks like the real deal. I've been hoping to see him play. All-State last year, just like Harper." Josiah Whitehawk's knowledge of

---

[18] ti\TŌKH\in

Idaho high school basketball astounded Coach McNeese.

"What do you think we should do against him?" Coach McNeese ventured. Glenns Ferry was heavily favored against the Southeastern Idaho League runners-up, the Malad Dragons.

"I guess we'll see in a few minutes," Josiah Whitehawk replied. Coach McNeese nodded and they settled back for the opening tip-off, two men crazy about basketball.

8:30 PM

Coach McNeese and Josiah Whitehawk drew a few stares from the nearly all-white crowd. Most people, though, remembered, "Oh, yeah. Lapwai just got done playing," and went about their business.

They watched Travis Wheatley tear apart the Dragon defense. Near the five-minute mark, with a 19 point lead, the Pilot coach finally took Wheatley out of the game.

"No use risking injury," Mr. Whitehawk commented.

Coach McNeese agreed. "That's about when I would've taken him out."

"Me, too," concurred the Nez Perce elder. "So...what are you going to do?"

"Well, we don't have to worry about the rest of the team." Josiah Whitehawk nodded. "I'm not too impressed with his passing. If we trap him at half-court, they're done."

Josiah Whitehawk pondered Coach McNeese's analysis.

"That should work..."

"Yes?" Coach McNeese encouraged.

"I think we can wear him down early. He's quick, but we got boys who can stay with him. Go to a two-two zone and stick one of those boys on ..."

"A Box-and-One?!" Coach McNeese exclaimed. "Why didn't I think of that?" he wondered to himself.

"Whatever you call it nowadays. Start with Jesse, then Jimmy. Or Billy. Heck, even Sonny. We all look alike, anyway. Sooyáapoo won't know who's on 'im." Josiah Whitehawk chuckled.

"And the other boys can slide over and help double-team," Coach McNeese added. "Coach Whitehawk, I owe you one." Josiah Whitehawk beamed. "I wonder if they can reprint the programs so I can put you down as an assistant coach?" Coach McNeese joked. "Say, can I give you a ride back to the hotel? My wife drove down. I have our car outside."

"You bet. But don't be taking me on no backroads." They both laughed and strolled out together, Mr. Whitehawk's moccasins scraping the oak floor, into the crisp early spring evening.

Lapwai Wildcats Versus Glenns Ferry Pilots

Practically every time Travis Wheatley brought the ball up-court he faced a different Lapwai defender. The more the Wildcat guards stifled

Wheatley, the more fun they had. Stopping the state's leading scorer became a contest. By halftime Wheatley was exhausted and ended up with half as many turnovers as points- 14 points. seven turnovers. Final score: Lapwai 47, Glenns Ferry 31. Sam pulled down 11 boards. Mike McNeese was unstoppable and finished with 28 points.

The Wildcats were playing for the state championship.

44

When something was broken, Big Ron Harper liked to fix it. The racial undercurrent of the Lapwai-Homevale game still gnawed at him. Minutes before the third/fourth place game between Glenns Ferry and New Plymouth, he left his seat and found Josiah Whitehawk.

"Excuse me...gotta minute?"

Josiah Whitehawk looked up in surprise and nodded toward the empty space beside him.

"I just wanted to tell you I'm sorry we had to see that kind of behavior last night. It was way out of line. Your boys play hard and deserve respect."

Josiah Whitehawk smiled and nodded. After a long pause he asked, "So...how you feel about our big game comin' up?" Big Ron relaxed. Case closed.

"Well, we whupped New Plymouth pretty good, but the way the McNeese kid played last night, it's anyone's ballgame."

"I think so, too," Josiah Whitehawk agreed. "He knows who he is now. He's content in his own skin with us 'Skins." Josiah Whitehawk chuckled to himself.

"I bet that's it. Boys need to feel they belong."

"So, who you like in this one?"

They spent the next two hours watching high school basketball and trading basketball stories. Big Ron recounted late-night bus rides through Camas Prairie blizzards in his playing days. Josiah recalled train trips up the Clearwater River, playing Gifford High School Friday night, sleeping in the basement gym around a pot-bellied wood stove, hopping back on the train for a noon game at Orofino, on to Greer for a Saturday night game, and back home in the wee hours Sunday morning. Their conversation finally ended when Glenns Ferry slipped by New Plymouth in the final 15 seconds for third place.

"It's been great visiting with you, Mr. Whitehawk. Again, I hope you all will forgive the ignorance of a few people. No hard feelings?"

"Oh, that was nothing. We're used to it. It brings out our warrior spirit, enit?" The Nez Perce elder smiled.

Big Ron Harper nodded and started to rise. "Good... Glad that's settled. You know, I...well, anyway, thank you." They exchanged the Nez Perce's customary light handshake.

"'Eehé," Mr. Whitehawk answered. He had just enough time to get a bag of popcorn before the 1972 Idaho A-3 Boys Basketball State Championship.

45

Four horses fled Thursday evening. Discovered downed fence rails, suspect the stallion. Located horses in a box canyon near the River. Six Nez Perce youth appeared on horseback, greatly assisted in recovery of all horses. Were fine riders, without use of saddle, and declined offers of reward.

From the Journal of J.H. Gwynn, Homesteader, Latah Valley Prairie, 1872

Goodwill existed between Latah Valley and Lapwai for 75 years. During the tuberculosis outbreak the Latah Valley Presbyterian Church Women's Circle baked monthly treats for the children at the sanatorium. Their town teams played spirited baseball games every Fourth of July in the twenties and thirties until World War Two. Somehow the familiarity between the pioneer community and the reservation town gradually faded.

Now it was back. Boys playing basketball. Nothing else. The way it was supposed to be.

46

1972 Idaho A-3 Basketball State Championship Game
Lapwai Wildcats Versus Latah Valley Falcons

Sam's frontcourt partner Mike grew up in small town high school gyms. For 17 years, his father's voice played in Mike's head. In his last high school basketball game, he remembered everything.

"Bounce-pass inside, cutter brushes off his man on the baseline, he's wide open underneath." Mike didn't even know how he knew what he knew. Tonight, instinctively, he sensed exactly what should happen everywhere on the court. He didn't have to think. Just play.

If he set a screen for Sonny, quickly re-set on the other side, Sonny would reverse for an easy lay-in. If Latah Valley didn't double-down on him, he could turn his shoulders, shield the ball with a raised inside arm, and Justin Murphy would have to foul or give up an easy jump-hook.

After Mike hit five-for-five inside and drew three fouls on Murphy, Coach Bradley collapsed his zone. The Wildcats picked up their ball movement and found the open shot outside. Three straight jumpers from Jesse and the passing lanes opened up again. Quick inlet pass, back out to Denny alone in the wing...swish. When the Falcons ran two defenders out on Denny, Luke was open on the other side of the court. Bank shot. Two points.

"You gotta call it next time, Lootz!" Denny laughed.

Still, the Falcons stayed close. Justin anxiously watched from the bench.

"Okay, I see what McNeese's doing. Don't let him get that arm up. Hook it, and get a hand in his face," Justin thought. He couldn't wait to get back in the game.

Ron Harper, Jr. respected how the Lapwai boys played basketball. He felt the same passion for the game. Tonight, he ignored his father's critical eyes. In <u>his</u> last high school game Ron, too, was playing for the love of it.

The feeling spread. After players dove for loose balls, they helped each other up. When someone finished off a well-executed play, the boys let each other know: "Good shot."

The Latah Valley players never really got what all the prejudice was about, anyway. Lapwai boys were a lot like themselves, really. They hung out, talked about girls, split a few beers on backroads sometimes, and played basketball.

After Justin tied the game at 57 on a perfect up-and-under lay-in, Jesse hollered to him, "You sure you're not Indian?!"

It was the best game ever. It was beautiful. It was spiritual.

With 13 seconds left in the game, the score 61 all, Sam and Rusty Bush got tied up and tumbled out of bounds. The crowd watched in horror as the boys flew headfirst toward the metal handrails bolted to the bleacher steps and awaited an awful head-splitting "Crack!" Inches from the railing's sharp edge, the boys suddenly, somehow, landed harmlessly on the floor.

The crowd gasped in unison. "What just happened?!" spread through the gym. Lapwai kids whispered to each other, "Long Shadow!"

"Chize! She saved both those sooyáapoos," Sonny whispered to Billy. They alone had seen the shadow's face before.

"Yeah. She must like what she sees."

"Jump ball!" hollered the referee.

Coach McNeese hastily signaled Billy to call time-out.

The boys huddled, turned toward Sam, and nodded. Looked like this ghost had a thing for Counts. She wouldn't let him down.

"What's going on?" Coach McNeese asked, bewildered. His eyes moved from face to face.

"Sam needs to take the last shot, Coach. It'll go," Billy promised.

For once, Coach McNeese hesitated. He appreciated Sam's hustle, his rebounding, his put-backs, but usually he'd set up Mike or Jesse out of time-out. But something about the looks on their faces...

"What the heck," he thought. "Sam misses, we go to overtime. Besides, Roy won't expect Sam to shoot."

"Okay. We need this jump ball." Sam nodded. "Jesse, Mike, set a double-screen down low. Sammy, you're going *between* them, and then we pinch in and shut off Bush." He turned to the guards. "He'll be wide open." Billy and Sonny nodded.

"Hey! We're having fun, right?!" The boys smiled. "They won't have time to get a shot off. It's all on us. Let's win this!"

Sam won the tip by a hand length. The ball fell into a pile of players. Billy dove and pushed the ball with outstretched fingertips to Sam just as he slipped through the double-screen.

Three seconds. Sam picked up the ball, squared his shoulders, and let go.

The basketball bounced twice on the front of the rim and dropped in. The Lapwai Wildcats were the Idaho A-3 State basketball champions.

The Indi'n Section went wild! The pep band played the school song three times through in the celebration. Nearly invisible in the shadows cast on the gymnasium wall, though, a young clarinet player sat trembling with fear, her horn resting on her lap. Only one person noticed her. Josiah Whitehawk.

"Did we go too far?" she worried. "Is this our way?"

Then two new doubts invaded Jessica's thoughts.

"I can't do this alone...why me?"

47

1846, 126 Years Earlier
Spalding's Mission to the Nez Perce

It was early spring. The mill trace was dry, for water diverted from Lapwai Creek was still many days away from powering Eliza's father's grist mill. Henry Spalding chose the confluence of Lapwai Creek and the Clearwater River for the site of his mission wisely. Soon, seeds for the coming year's crops would be sown in the rich soil.

Eight-year-old Eliza and a girl the missionaries called Suzie hid in the banks of the mill trace and braided buttercups into Suzie's waist-length hair.

"You are my best friend, Suzie," Eliza quietly stated.

Suzie glanced in every direction before whispering, "Call me Sayáq'ic húukux. 'Pretty Hair'."

Eliza and Suzie rose to their knees and scanned the mission ground for Eliza's father. Suddenly Henry Spalding appeared on the front porch of the missionary house. His stern face was angry, and

Suzie glimpsed a willow switch behind his back. Suzie grabbed Eliza's arm, pulled her to the ground, and flung her shawl over Eliza's blonde hair. They waited a few moments and then peeked over the crest of the mill trace. Eliza looked into Suzie's eyes and said, "I will always love you, Sayáq'ic húukux."

"And I will always protect you," answered Pretty Hair. Together they opened the sharp blade of a small pocket knife. They bravely cut the tips of the first fingers of their right hands and squeezed tiny drops of blood together.

"Now we are sisters," Eliza declared.

"Forever," added Pretty Hair.

PART TWO
Home

**Indian Nations Participating in the First Annual
Warm Springs All-Indian High School Basketball
Tournament**

48

Back home, their trophy in place, the boys kept playing basketball. On the court they were still state champions. They weren't ready to let that go. Every day at 3:15 it was either the high school gym, the Pi-Nee-Waus, or, in glorious early spring warmth, the elementary school playground, throwing down thunderous dunks on eight-foot baskets in the shadow of their childhood.

Sam was obsessed. One day in Senior English, drawing basketballs on his *Great Expectations* notes, he got a wild idea.

"I wonder if Ron Harper wants to come down and play? Spring sports haven't started yet. Up on the Palouse, I bet it's still too wet out on the baseball field. He could bring down his cousin. Maybe Rusty Bush. It would be awesome."

It only took two random phone calls to track down Ron's number. Ron thought it sounded like an excellent idea.

So Wednesday afternoon at four o'clock, the 1972 Idaho State A-3 Championship Game rivals met again. But this time was very different.

The boys split up: Mike, Ron, Luke, Rusty, and Billy against Justin, Jesse, Jimmy, Sam, and Sonny.

It was, indeed, awesome. With, let's say, 'lax' defense, the shots flew. The boys went crazy when Mike, Justin, and then Sam all dunked breakaways.

Ron felt free beyond his father's control. After seeing Jesse hit Justin underneath with two slick no-look passes, he did the same to Mike. He never would've done that at home!

A small crowd gathered. Something special was happening- Lapwai and Latah Valley boys playing Indi'n ball together. The old folks thought, "These new sooyáapoos were born to do this. This team could beat Lewiston."

Julia and Jessica finished pow-wow dance practice at five. "Let's go watch 'em play," suggested Julia, and the girls perched on the bleachers.

Ron wanted to give the crowd a show. He dribbled down-court, spun around Billy, and flicked the ball over the rim with a backward lay-in. He caught Julia's eye and smiled.

After two games to a hundred points, the boys finally had enough.

Ron, Justin, and Rusty made two more trips to Lapwai. The girls found reasons to pass their afternoons at the Buildin', and Ron zoomed in on Julia.

"Okay, man, what are you doing?" he asked himself. "Basketball's one thing, but an Indian girlfriend? I don't think so. Besides, she's going out with Mike. She is really cool, but my world's not ready for that yet."

So the three Latah Valley boys thanked their new friends and said, "See you in baseball." The boys thought differently about Lapwai now. They were changed by the events of this basketball season.

Ron, Justin, and Rusty showered, stepped into the Pi-Nee-Waus Café, and ordered large sodas to go. A sign caught their eyes- *Fry Bread Friday*. They each bought two and stepped outside.

"Háamt'ic, sooyáapoo!" Ron hollered to Justin as he got behind the wheel of his pickup to head back up Coyote Grade. Two elders having a smoke nearby looked up and laughed.

They had also learned some good Indian words to use on friends.

49

Denny's father, Dennis Senior, the Wildcat Boosters president, suggested the club present the boys with mementos of their great season at the basketball banquet. They already had class rings, so that was out. They didn't need another medal on their letterman's jackets. With awards for band, Future Farmers of America, football, and the many other activities small-school students do, they already sounded like walking sleigh bells. It needed to be something *different*.

"Something lasting they can carry with them after the memories fade." He wandered in and out of stores in downtown Lewiston and found himself in Lolo Sporting Goods Store.

"I've been wanting to get Denny a deer rifle, anyway," he thought. "I think I'll just look around here for a moment."

Dennis's eyes wandered past racks of rifles, dusty big game mounts, and outdated calendar paintings of western scenes to boxes of shells and bullets in display cases near the front window. On the lowest shelf, bone handles and silver casings of rows of hunting and pocket knives reflected the late afternoon sun.

"That's it!" He stooped to inspect the knives more closely.

"Hmmm...ten players, two managers...be nice to get Ray and Earl one, too," Dennis calculated. "We probably want something nice, but small...say, two blades...good for small jobs, like cutting rope or maybe fishing line. We should get the varsity cheerleaders something, too. Vicky can help me with that later."

The sales clerk laid one of the smaller models on the countertop. Dennis saw that "1972 State Champs" would fit nicely on one end and "Lapwai Wildcats" on the other.

"I'll need fourteen of them," he notified the surprised clerk. Just then, inspiration struck. "Make that fifteen."

"A token-of-appreciation for the Wildcats' Number One Fan. Brilliant, if I don't mind saying so myself," Dennis thought.

Lolo Sporting Goods received a special shipment on Wednesday. Dennis rushed the knives to A Plus Trophies for engraving, and in velvet-lined wooden cases, he thought they made very nice gifts.

50

Dennis, the players, managers, coaches, and special guest Josiah Whitehawk posed for a group picture before opening the small packages wrapped in silver paper. Sam's jaw dropped. In his hand lay an exact copy of May's knife. He had forgotten his promise.

Sam quietly rode home with his parents.

"Everything okay back there, Sammy?" his father asked.

"Oh, I'm just thinking. It's been a crazy winter." His parents nodded in agreement.

Sam folded his coat into a pillow and rested his head against the window.

"May's knife...the whole team has one now. What does that mean?" Sam wondered. They crossed the Clearwater and drove past the shadows of Spalding Park. "We need to get to Oregon and return May's knife to her brother somehow. But maybe we don't go alone."

51

When Josiah and Ida Whitehawk drove to Lewiston for the basketball banquet, Jessica stayed home with her little sisters. They watched cartoons, ate some cereal, and stepped outside. Brown, muddy water reached the front steps, but Jessica could see the nearby flooding creek had crested in the night and their house was safe this time.

The little girls dashed ahead. "Jessie, let's play!" They joyfully stomped through the ankle deep water covering their driveway.

"Wait!" Jessica shouted. "Come back and get your rubber boots on." Her sisters obediently hurried back inside, leaving muddy footprints in their wake. Jessica smiled and sighed.

"I probably did the same thing when I was little," she laughed to herself. Lapwai Creek had always been a companion. When she was ten, Grandfather taught her to gaff the Coho salmon making their way to the spawning grounds upstream. She learned how to set the hook at just the right moment and how to land the catch safely on shore.

Jessica spent scorching summer days at the swimming hole near her house called Overhead, where Lapwai Creek reached its deepest. They jumped off the concrete bridge there and felt their toes sink into the mud.

"You wanna go look at the creek?" she asked her sisters. Their excited smiles told her "Yes!"

They held hands and climbed the bank through bull thistles, locust tree saplings, and coyote weed to stare into the churning monster that was Lapwai Creek in high water. Jagged two-by-fours and plywood swooshed past. Waves slapped the shore and ripped apart the bank.

Jessica felt the water call her. She gripped her sisters' wrists so tightly their skin turned white. She stepped into the creek and pulled them in with her.

"Where are we going?" whispered a frightened voice. Jessica turned with a smile the little girls had never seen before. A shadow in the water behind her refracted into a thousand pieces.

"We're going home." In seconds, the current caught Jessica's sisters and spun them in circles. Jessica felt her fingers let go and watched the little girls swirl helplessly downstream. Plunging into the torrent, she desperately grabbed one tiny hand, and together they were swept onto a log caught on the bridge's pier.

She quickly hoisted her sobbing sister to safety. "Stay here!" she commanded. "I'll come back for you!" Her sister simply nodded as tears rolled down her face. Jessica leaned into the current and finally stepped ashore.

She ran along the shoreline, frantically searching for her other sister. At last she found her, clinging to a sturdy branch midstream. Seeing her big sister coming to save her, she reached out.

"Hang on! Don't let go! I'll get you!" Branch by branch, Jessica carefully made her way through the current, until she at last reached her sister.

"What should I do?" a tiny voice pleaded.

"Grab onto me!" Jessica shouted over the flooding creek's roar. Eyes wide with fright, Jessica's sister did as she was told.

The brown water eddied around the two, and Jessica let it push them toward shore. Wearied arms squeezed tightly around her neck. Jessica's feet finally touched solid ground. She wrapped her arms around her sister's legs, lifted her out of the water, and they hurried to their sister still waiting, frightened, in the floodwater.

Jessica gingerly retraced her way along the trunks of uprooted cottonwood trees, balancing with one hand on the concrete bridge, now only inches above the swollen river. "Get on me!" she yelled. Her sister climbed onto her back, and moments later they were all together again on the bank. They huddled in silence and stared at the debris speeding past.

"This cannot happen," Jessica resolved as the little ones shivered in her arms. "I will try to be who you want me to be, May, but my sisters cannot be in danger again. I must first protect them."

She looked into their trusting eyes and smiled. "Now let's go home." This time, Jessica's sisters smiled back.

52

March 4, 1972

Late Saturday morning Jesse and Sam stood at the Pi-Nee-Waus gym entrance. A new poster taped to the right-side door read, "First Annual High School Pow-Wow and Basketball Tournament March 10-11, 1972. Cash prizes for boys and girls fast-and-fancy and traditional. Trophies awarded to first and second place basketball teams. High school Indian youth are invited to participate."

Three words on the bottom of the page stunned Sam. "*Warm Springs, Oregon.*" A moment later, Sam started plotting.

"We should do this, enit?" he suggested to Jesse.

"You're forgetting one thing, Counts."

"What's that?"

"You're not Indian."

"It says *participate.* Us white guys could just watch."

"You'd go to a basketball tournament, sit on the bench, and just watch?" Jesse asked.

"Yeah, why not? It'd be fun to go. Road trip, like State."

"Wouldn't have anything to do with Jessica?" Jesse teased.

"She's going?" Sam hadn't thought of that.

"What is Jessica's part in returning May's knife?" he wondered.

"Yeah, she'll probably go. She and Julia. It's like the start of pow-wow season. They gotta check out the competition, enit? And Jessica has family there."

Again, Sam had to collect himself. In a moment, he calmly asked, "Really? How do you know that?"

"What do you mean, 'How do I know that?' I'm Nez Perce. We know everybody else's families. Jessica's Nez Perce relatives in Warm Springs go way back, but we never forget." Jesse punched Sam on the shoulder. "You know Indi'ns are tight, enit?"

Sam nodded. He also sensed that more discoveries lay ahead before all the pieces fell in place to help May, a girl Sam was beginning to consider a friend, find peace.

If he only knew...

11:30 AM

The other boys soon arrived and gathered around the poster.

"Counts wants to go to this tournament. And just watch," Jesse added.

Sam caught Denny's eye. "It's in Warm Springs."

Denny shrugged a "So?"

"Warm Springs...Oregon," Sam repeated.

Denny finally caught on. "Oh! Yeah, I'd like to go. I'm okay with just shooting around and then watching the games. I'd like to see some other teams play, see how good they are."

Jesse nodded. "I bet the Crows are wicked good." Every spring the Nez Perce Tribe hosted an all-Indian basketball tournament. Many years the Crow Nation team from Montana faced the hosts in the championship games.

"Yeah, well, you, Billy, Sonny, Junior, Jimmy..." Denny paused. "I hate to be the one to tell you this, Jesse, but you guys are a little on the short side. Crows are, like, super tall. You need a big man."

"We got one."

53

Tony Jackson

For thousands of years, several confederated bands of the Nez Perce existed in the region where Idaho, Washington, and Oregon now meet, including areas around Lapwai, Kamiah, the Grand Ronde and Snake rivers confluence, and Tsceminicum.

In 1860, gold was discovered near present day Pierce, Idaho. Steamboats laden with newcomers chugged up the Columbia and Snake rivers from Portland, Oregon. More strikes followed. Fortune seekers embarked for the gold fields from the Confluence, where the Clearwater flowed into the

Snake. By 1872, nine years after Lewiston became Idaho's first territorial capital in 1863, few Nez Perce remained Where the Rivers Meet, or *Tsceminicum.*

Clearwater Timber Company opened in Lewiston in 1927 and later became part of Potlatch Forests. The name *Potlatch,* Chinook trade jargon for 'to give away,' proved bitterly ironic. Traditional forms of subsistence were disappearing. In the imminence of a changing world many Nez Perce went to work at the lumber and pulp mills there.

Some Nez Perce families braved the bigotry they encountered in Lewiston in order to live closer to work. They visited family in nearby Lapwai often and maintained tribal ties at pow-wows and encampments.

Tony Jackson's grandparents were two of those early 'urban' Indians. Jesse, Billy, and Sonny last played basketball with him at the Pi-Nee-Waus two years earlier. Lately, Tony had grown more comfortable with his white teammates at Lewiston High School and didn't much want to go out to the reservation. At six foot five, he started his senior year on the Bengal varsity.

It was time for Tony Jackson to get back to his roots.

54

Just one call from his cousin Junior got Tony to the Pi-Nee-Waus. He planned to go out soon anyway to see if the boys were that good. He was tired of hearing about Lapwai's state championship, how they could beat Lewiston. Yeah, he'd show them.

He found they really were that good. They played with a selflessness Tony rarely felt. Lapwai boys *shared* the court. There was a *connection*.

Tony loved being part of it. It filled an empty space in his life. In Lewiston, he often felt he had to prove himself. Sometimes his Lewiston teammates forgot that Tony, being fairly light-skinned, was Indian. He laughed off jokes about Indians that really weren't that funny. It seemed sometimes Tony himself almost forgot who he was.

Here he could be himself. The boys welcomed him home.

55

Monday, March 6, 1972

The Warm Springs Inter-Tribal Pow-Wow Committee included entry forms with each poster announcing the First Annual Warm Springs High School Pow-Wow and Basketball Tournament. Sonny and Billy picked one up at the Pi-Nee-Waus office and studied the rules. The first paragraph, of course, declared that all participants must be enrolled tribal members.

The second paragraph explained that high school interscholastic activities association guidelines applied. Rule Number One: "Teams may not wear the uniforms of their high schools."

"No problem," said Billy. "We'll just borrow the Nation's." The Warm Springs event was scheduled around other Western pow-wows and basketball tournaments.

Rule Two stopped the boys cold. "Coaching staff currently employed by any public or private school district may not be associated with practices or competition." That meant Coach McNeese, and even Coach Guerreros, were out.

"So we need to find a coach," Sonny concluded. "Shouldn't be too hard. Half of Lapwai think they're basketball coaches."

"Yeah, but he has to be able to take time off work. Or maybe not working, like an older guy," Billy added.

"He should be titóoqan," Billy stated. Sonny nodded. "Somebody who won't try to change us. Somebody who watched us play."

Sonny and Billy recalled the Indi'n Section. The image of a serene but passionate elder sitting on the court-side row, eating popcorn from an upturned ten gallon hat, popped into both boys' minds. They smiled, gave each other a quick fist-tap, and said together, "Josiah Whitehawk."

4:00 PM

:The others thought it was a brilliant choice. They were in the high school gym locker room changing clothes. Even Terry was there. They expected Tony in half an hour.

"He'll let us run," Jesse figured. "And he really knows a lot. He gave me a good tip about my jump shot. He'll be really excited to be asked." Jesse remembered when Sam and he visited Mr. Whitehawk a couple of months ago.

"You're right. We can run all we want," Jimmy agreed. "But we don't hardly have any subs. Me, Sonny, Billy, Jesse, Junior, Tony...it's not like during the season. We need another Indian."

Everyone turned toward Terry, sitting at the end of the locker room bench with his hand raised.

"Terry, you don't have to raise your hand to speak!" Denny laughed. Terry kept his hand in the air. Denny shook his head and said, "Yes? Terry?"

Terry cleared his throat. "How about me?"

"What?!" the boys shouted in unison.

"My mom's family's from Oklahoma," Terry explained. "My grandmother's half Cherokee. My mom told me it's enough to be a member of the tribe if I wanted."

The boys burst out laughing. "Terry! I always knew you were holding out on us!" Billy said and gave the top of Terry's fist a tap. Terry responded with a shy smile.

"Okay, then. Seven players ought to be enough. One Indi'n carload!" laughed Jesse.

So the roster was set: four Nez Perce, a Nez Perce/Sioux, a Seneca, a very light-skinned Cherokee, and a cheering section made up of four white friends.

All the boys needed now was a coach.

Josiah Whitehawk's answer surprised Sonny and Billy.

"All you boys come here tomorrow after school," was all he said.

The boys arrived at Josiah Whitehawk's place at four o'clock the next day. He met them outside his front door, his dog by his side. Sam scratched the old mutt under his chin.

"The rocks are hot," declared Mr. Whitehawk.

The boys followed the Nez Perce elder around back, past several old cars and a firewood lean-to. Behind a stand of bull thistle, a thin pillar of smoke rose. The thistle, hackberry trees, and chokecherry bushes indicated that a small spring seeped from a nearby rock outcropping. The boys, except Mike and Terry, knew what lay around the path's next corner. Terry was in for his first formal lesson on being Indian.

A small stock tank caught the trickling hillside spring water. An iron pipe near the top of the tank sent the overflow on its way to Garden Creek. An old tin bowl waited on a flat, mossy rock ledge. Later, after their sweat, Josiah Whitehawk and the boys would use it to douse themselves with the ice-cold water from the stock tank.

A small hand-welded sheet metal stove used to heat the sweathouse rocks emitted the fragrance of burning locust tree leaves. Nearby, grey and brown blankets and gunny sacks covered a rustic five-foot high rounded structure.

"You sooyáapoo boys ever gone sweatin'?" Mr. Whitehawk asked with a grin. In fact, Luke and Denny had been to several of the more-frequented sweathouses hidden up gulches, near hillside edges, and behind cottonwood and locust groves along Lapwai Creek. Sam had been to all of them with Jesse.

"Uncle, you been keeping your sweathouse a secret, enit?" Sonny joked.

"This one's just for special occasions. Invitation only," Mr. Whitehawk chuckled and then added seriously, "We need to get ready for Warm Springs. Get our hearts right."

"I guess this means we have a coach," Billy whispered to Sonny.

The boys folded their clothes into neat piles on a long weather-worn wooden bench. A woven basket held a dozen towels. Inside the sweathouse, six stones glowed. An aged enameled bowl was set beside them.

Josiah Whitehawk neared the sweathouse, chanted, "Hyaah!" and a passageway into the shadows appeared in a space between two newly-parted blankets. Another elder, his skin glistening in the steamy fog, sat back down and solemnly nodded to the boys.

Josiah Whitehawk entered first. His long hair hung loose. He eased himself onto a thick mat covering the ground. One-by-one the boys hunkered through the opening, circled the steaming rocks, and wordlessly sat. Their knees pressed against one another's in the darkness.

"Jesse, you wanna do the honors?" asked Mr. Whitehawk. Jesse leaned forward, scooped a handful of spring water from the bowl in front of him, and sprinkled the glowing rocks. A thick layer of steam rose.

Terry had never known such completely sweltering heat. He felt his bones melt. His breathing came in short gasps. His mind cleared until he was aware of only this: his body in this small space, surrounded by his teammates, now faintly visible in the amber-colored light cast by the hot rocks. He was here. Nothing else mattered. Almost.

His doubts returned. Would people say he didn't belong? Sure, he was 'part Indian.' What did that mean? Would he really step onto the court in Warm Springs?

56

Tuesday, March 6, 1972

Sam walked out of the Buildin' into a cool rain. Spring was around the corner. Rhubarb would soon flourish in the alley behind Aunt Milly's house where Sam and Gordy once played. Rainy days always reminded Sam of those times, tromping the hills around Lapwai in grey mornings and then playing upstairs with army men during heavy afternoon downpours.

He had lost track of Gordy. He hadn't visited Aunt Milly for a while, either. Maybe he'd go over right now.

Sam approached Norman Green Bomb and saw he had a passenger. He recognized her shoulder-length light brown hair and smiled.

"'Bout time, Counts. I need a ride home. I don't want to get all wet," Vicky stated.

"Oh, Vicky! What an unexpected pleasure! Would you like a ride?" Sam feigned surprise.

"Whatever. Let's go. I gotta talk to you. You're in trouble."

Sam raised his eyebrows and took his hand off the key left in the ignition. "Okay, I'll bite. What is it?"

"So, what's your plan?" Vicky wasted no time. "You got everybody all excited to go to Warm Springs. Terry's all worried about what he's going to do when he gets there." Vicky paused, and Sam sensed, for once, she was serious. Sam would never mean to upset his soft-spoken sophomore teammate.

After a long pause, the conversation returned to the back-and-forth play Sam and Vicky were used to.

"So you're going to Warm Springs," Vicky repeated. "Then what? You going to walk around and ask every elder you see if he had a sister 60 years ago named May?"

Sam shrugged his shoulders. Vicky was right.

"I told you before, you need my ingenious mind for planning. No offense, Counts, but you're just like every other guy. 'Just see what happens next.' That's why I'm going to Warm Springs with you."

"What?!" A moment later, though, he laughed. Vicky stopped surprising Sam long ago.

"Yes, I'm going with you, and we're going to find May's brother, and we're going to give him back the knife. And May will be at peace. But we're not waiting until we get there to start looking for him."

"Wait... How are you getting there? Where you staying? What are you thinking?!" Sam managed to counter. "How long has she been planning this?" he wondered.

"It's getting cold. Let's turn on some heat."

Sam started his pickup and turned the heater on full blast. The defroster cleared the fog from the windshield and Sam and Vicky watched rivulets of raindrops make tracks down the curved edge of the windshield.

"It's all worked out, Counts."

"Of course," Sam thought.

"I'm going over with Jessica's mom. Julia and Jessica are going to dance, of course. We're staying at Jessica's aunt's place. Julia thought I could tell Mom and Dad that they need help with their pow-wow dresses and their hair. It's all set."

Sam smiled. Of course Vicky was going. Vicky's memory of watching May's shadow walk down the canal from the children's graveyard haunted her. Vicky felt May's sorrow, her longing to say goodbye to her family. Vicky wanted to help May find rest.

Sam knew she would always be there for him, too. "May and I are lucky to have Vicky for a friend," he thought.

Sam steered Norman Green Bomb toward Vicky's house. "So, how do we start?"

"Chize, Counts, don't you ever watch TV? Mannix? Columbo? Ironside? We talk to people who might know something. Do you know if anyone in Lapwai actually knew May?"

Sam swerved and made a wide U-turn.

"Where are we going?!"

"We're going to see May's best friend."

"Now you're getting it, Counts!" Soon, the old Studebaker pickup turned onto a familiar street at the base of a bare, stony hill.

As Sam and Vicky pulled up in front of Aunt Milly's white, two-story home, they noticed a front room curtain part a few inches. Before Sam and Vicky even stepped onto the front porch, Aunt Milly was waiting in the open doorway.

"Sammy! Vicky! I thought I might see you two today." She embraced each of them in turn.

"I heard you two are both going to Warm Springs." Sam looked first at Vicky and then back to Aunt Milly, perplexed. "Oh, yes, I learned from Julia about Vicky going with Julia and Jessica last week at the Pi-Nee-Waus. You're behind the times, Redwing," Aunt Milly chuckled. Teaching the girls traditional dance brought a new light to her eyes. Beside her, Vicky smiled.

"So come in and sit down. I baked a pie for the occasion."

"Gordy's favorite," Sam added to himself. Sam and Vicky took their places on the old, comfortable sofa, covered with a blue and red patterned Pendleton blanket, next to Aunt Milly's chair.

"So, how can I help you?" Aunt Milly asked, handing Sam and Vicky each a slice of lemon meringue pie. Sam was surprised at Aunt Milly's directness. No small talk about school or family this time.

"She knows we're up to something," Sam thought. So Sam got right to the point.

"We want to find May's brother. We want to hand him the knife."

Aunt Milly nodded and was soon lost in memory. In a few moments, though, she broke the silence.

"May's brother has been lost for some years. He's going to be hard to find. We can't wait 'til we get there to start looking for him."

Vicky turned to Sam with a smug grin. "See?" she mouthed. Sam just shook his head.

"We need somebody who can..." Aunt Milly stopped mid-sentence.

"What?!" Sam and Vicky exclaimed together.

"Gordy!"

"Gordy?"

"Yes! Gordy!" Aunt Milly repeated. "He lives there now! His mom and them settled down there last year. They live down to Warm Springs now!"

Aunt Milly continued. "You remember, Redwing, Gordy's studying to go into law enforcement. The tribal police there been teaching him. He works three afternoons a week. That's his afternoon high school class. They been giving him lots of responsibility. He'll be a real good policeman." Aunt Milly added quietly, "Just like his grandfather."

"He could start looking for May's brother!" Sam realized.

"He'd like to do it, too," Aunt Milly agreed. "You know, Redwing, Gordy 'fessed up on the phone about the knife couple days ago, him giving you something that wasn't his. He did a good thing, admittin' it. He's a good boy." Aunt Milly was very proud of her sister's son she helped raise.

"That's excellent!" Vicky exclaimed. She bounced with excitement. "He can access the FBI files and cross-reference information with tribal records... Was May's brother a veteran? He'll need to check VA records, and..."

"Okay, Columbo, we get it," Sam laughed. He placed his hand on her knee for a moment to slow her down.

Aunt Milly smiled. She liked the funny, energetic white girl. Vicky spent almost as much time at the Pi-Nee-Waus dance classes as the Indian girls.

Moments later, Sam caught on. "Wait a second... Auntie, did you say _we_ can't wait to look for May's brother?"

"Sammy, you really need to keep up. I'm going, too."

"You are?!"

"Oh, yes. I'm an advisor for Julia and them," Aunt Milly beamed with pride. "I got a ride with Jessica's mom." Sam glanced toward Vicky, who just nodded.

"Besides..." Aunt Milly's face became serious. A trace of bittersweet sadness crept into her moist eyes. "...I want to say goodbye to May."

"And I must see that she leaves," she added to herself.

May's words came back to her. "I will always be with you."

"I will never forget you, May," thought Aunt Milly. "But you cannot be here any longer. You must let go of Jessica."

57

Thursday, March 2, 1972

The boys' last practice before the Warm Springs tournament was a full-court scrimmage. Earl Guerreros refereed, and Mrs. McNeese ran the clock. About 50 spectators gathered by the middle of the first quarter.

Sam felt uncomfortable at first with the two squads divided down racial lines. It wasn't the way they did things. But as they traded baskets and he heard the mostly-Indian crowd cheering the play of all the boys on the court, Sam relaxed.

The Indian boys obviously had a bond, but a kinship existed among the white boys, too. Growing up on the reservation set them apart from other white boys. It was part of who they were.

The score stayed close, like countless games on the playground courts, but in the last minute Jesse and Sonny hit back-to-back jumpers off nice picks by Tony, and the Indian boys won by three. Fine with Sam.

"Good hustle, boys," Coach Whitehawk said in the post-game huddle. "We want to do the same things at Warm Springs. Set the tempo. Good ball movement, but if you got your man one-on-one, take him. It was a good workout. Did you have fun?" The boys all nodded. "That's good. That's what it's all about. Now meet me out front after you shower."

The boys looked at each other, puzzled. Another sweat? They wondered what their new coach was up to now. They knew in some ways Josiah Whitehawk belonged to another time. They couldn't wait to see what he had planned next.

Harriet Whitebird

Twenty minutes later, the boys stood on the Pi-Nee-Waus parking lot. There, with the sliding door open, Earl Guerreros in the driver's seat, awaited the Appaloosa Express. Spray-painted black spots covered the back third of the tribe's old school bus, repainted a light brown.

"Háamt'ic, boys! You gave me a workout. I want to eat some good Indi'n food," shouted Mr. Guerreros. The boys piled onto the small, rattly bus. Josiah Whitehawk ambled up the bus steps to join them.

"We have a special meal waiting for us, boys," Coach Whitehawk announced. "Some real traditional food fixed by ladies who cook old-style. It reminds us we represent not just ourselves, and our families, but our past, too. I know you'll make Lapwai proud the way you play the game and treat people with respect, the Indian way." Coach

Whitehawk had the team's full attention. "I know you will also show respect to the ladies who prepared this dinner in our honor," Josiah Whitehawk concluded. The boys nodded.

The Appaloosa Express stopped in front of the Methodist Mission Church nine minutes later. The boys followed Mr. Guerreros and Coach Whitehawk into the small greystone church's fellowship hall. Three elderly women, white aprons over their flower-print dresses, stood behind the kitchen serving counter and greeted the boys with warm smiles. One-by-one the boys passed in front of the large opening between the hall and the kitchen and said, "Qe'ciyéw'yew'" to their hosts. They formed a semi-circle as Harriet Whitebird explained each dish.

"So we have some fry bread for you boys. Put lots of honey on it, it's real good. In this pot is some elk, slow-cooked the old way. Here we have some baked salmon caught just two days ago up to Rapid River. Next is something you sooyáapoo boys may not of had. You Indi'n boys better had some, or I'm gonna have to talk to your moms about it: some traditional dried corn. Different from what you're used to. Of course, here are some roots. And last, but not least, we have a real old-time dish. Goes way back to the days when the Nez Perce had to just make it through the hard winters some years. This is what they ate when there was no game, no nothing."

Mrs. Whitebird continued. "When a Nez Perce hunting party found Lewis and Clark and them starving on Lolo Pass, this is what saved them. It's *hóopop*[19], made from the moss from pine trees." The boys again thanked the cooks.

Jesse and Sonny smiled when Mrs. Higeagle finished. The other boys, even Terry, knew about hóopop. Everyone except Mike.

The boys formed a line behind the two coaches. Jesse and Sonny placed themselves on either side of Mike. As they neared the end of the line of bowls and platters of traditional Nez Perce food, Jesse coaxed, "Mike, make sure you try some hóopop. It's real good."

"Nobody hardly ever fixes it," Sonny added. "It takes a long time to do it right."

"Okay, I guess. Sure," Mike answered skeptically. He dipped the serving spoon into the thick concoction.

The boys wandered over to a long line of tables and sat down. After Mike tried a few bites of fry bread, salmon, and elk, Jesse stopped him.

"You don't want to get too full before you try some hóopop, Mike. You might want seconds before it's all gone." The others eyed Mike. He poked the black paste the consistency of tar into the tip of his spoon. As he raised it to his lips, he noticed that everybody watched him.

"Something's going on," Mike realized.

---

[19] HŌ\pōp

He took a bite. It was the most bitter food he had ever tasted. It was as if someone stuffed a handful of soggy weeds down his throat. The boys all grinned.

"They wanted to know if I would try it," Mike thought. "They been testing me all year, and I think I've done pretty good."

Suddenly he realized, "I'm glad we came here. I know what other people think of Lapwai. These are my friends now. If this is another test I have to pass to belong here, let's make it the last one."

Mike controlled the urge to spit the morsel of hóopop into his napkin and smiled broadly. "Mmmmm, this is so good!" He lowered his spoon to his plate and filled it to the brim. He took a large bite of hóopop and savored it with sounds of pure delight.

"What's wrong with you guys? Don't you like it? I'm going to finish what I have and see if there's any more. You better eat up fast, or there won't be any left. I might take it all." Mike paused. "Unless it's too much for you."

The smiles dropped from Jesse's and Sonny's faces, and they choked down the hóopop on their plates. They had to admit: they asked for it.

Like in the state championship game a month earlier, when he shut down one of the top high school players in the state of Idaho, it was game time for Mike.

"Isn't this great?! That hóopop, I don't believe I've ever had anything so tasty before!" He left his seat and sauntered to the serving counter.

"Qe'ciyéw'yew', ladies. Everything is delicious. Do you think I could have some more hóopop?" Mike asked the amused elders.

Mike was on a roll. "Don't let up now," he told himself. "Show 'em what you got." He wandered from table to table, plate in hand, eating hóopop and exclaiming its virtues.

"What's wrong, Counts? No hóopop? Not used to it?" Sam glanced up at Mike's grinning face and reluctantly started in on his hóopop.

"Yeah, Mike, it's really good," Sam managed to sputter after a few bites.

The other boys took their cues from Sam to avoid Mike's harangue.

"I bet they don't have anything this good in Oklahoma, enit, Terry?" He walked over to Tony.

"Good thing you didn't stay in Lewiston, enit, Tony?"

Nothing could stop Mike now. After he was sure all his teammates were 'enjoying' their hóopop, Mike finally sat back down. He turned toward Coach Guerreros and Josiah Whitehawk and raised a spoonful of hóopop in salute. The two coaches' shoulders shook in suppressed laughter.

Finally, the hóopop gone, along with most of the other dishes, the team thanked their hosts a final time and loaded the Appaloosa Express to return to the Pi-Nee-Waus. Once there, Mike bid farewell to his quietly suffering teammates and plopped behind the wheel of his family's sedan.

"I won," Mike said aloud once he was alone. His stomach gurgled. Nobody should eat that much hóopop. "Now if I can just make it home so I can lie down and die..."

58

Friday, March 10, 1972

"What the heck?!" Denny shouted to no one in particular. "Where's Counts?! He's usually early for things."

Coach Guerreros spun in the driver's seat of the Appaloosa Express. "Denny, maybe you should go to his house and see what's going on. We need to leave. This ol' Indi'n bus can't go over 50 miles an hour. We gotta make it to Warm Springs sometime this week."

At 9:30 AM Sam's mother shouted upstairs, "Time to get up, Sam! Your bus leaves at ten, right?! You packed yet?!"

Sam jumped to his feet, dashed into the shower, and then dressed. He was usually the first person at school events. Before home games, he liked to stand at mid-court in the empty and silent gym before the crowds and noise.

Sam jammed extra clothes into his blue and white "Lapwai Wildcats" duffel bag along with a few bathroom items. He started downstairs, but at the last moment remembered...the knife! He reached inside a pair of dress socks in the back of the bottom dresser drawer. May's knife was gone.

"Háamt'ic, Jessica!" Ida Whitehawk shouted. "We got to get to Warm Springs by four for registration. We still gotta pick up Vicky and Julia and Aunt Milly. We're not runnin' on Indi'n time today."

Jessica was almost finished. Extra clothes were packed in a brown suitcase waiting by her bedroom door. She carefully folded her pow-wow outfits, passed down from generation to generation. Each new dancer added part of herself to the regalia. Last year, Ida helped Jessica bead tiny blue camas blossoms (Jessica's favorite flower) on the sleeves of her fast-and-fancy dress.

Jessica thought of her mother, her grandmother, and her great-grandmother wearing the dresses as girls. Rings of sweat stained the soft leather, a reminder of summer pow-wows held long ago under a scorching western sun. She pictured clouds of dust stirred by Nez Perce, Umatilla, Cayuse, Yakama, and Warm Springs dancers, holding onto the old ways in the face of change. She imagined her ancestors as teens, spending warm evenings flirting, while the older folks played stick games until the first light of dawn.

Jessica remembered Aunt Suzie, her great, great-grandmother's sister, whose Indian name was now hers; the one with the long, beautiful hair who fell in love at a pow-wow with a handsome young

Warm Springs man and made a new life far from home.

"It's a little different now." She thought of Sam. She liked being with him. She could be herself. She was proud that he organized the boys into a team for Warm Springs. For May. She smiled thinking of him watching her dance.

"I think I'll go over to the Buildin' and see him before he goes," she thought.

Folding the arms of her jingle dress into an ancient strap suitcase, she felt a hard lump in the waist pocket. She removed the heavy dress and laid it full-length on her bed. She reached into the pocket and removed a small white knife. Jessica froze. "Does she believe in me now...or is she just testing my strength?" Aunt Milly's words came back to her.

"It's good Redwing holds the knife for now. This power object could weaken you until you are ready to help May let go of the knife."

"Is she setting' me up?" Jessica worried. "What does May <u>want</u>?" Jessica shivered when she realized what she had to do.

Mike skidded across the graveled corner of the Pi-Nee-Waus parking lot. "Slow down, man! We're okay. Counts's house is like a minute from here, anyway." Mike nodded and calmed down.

Denny let himself in the back door and climbed the stairway to Sam's room, like he had done a thousand times before. Carol Evans raised her head a moment when she heard the thumping footsteps and then returned to her ironing.

Denny burst into Sam's room. Sam was dumping the contents of his dresser drawers onto his bed.

"What the...?!"

"Denny! I can't find the knife! Go look in my closet, inside my shoes or something." Panic spread across Sam's face.

"Counts. Take it easy." Denny gripped his friend's arm. "It's not lost. I know you. You check it every night, right?" Sam nodded. "I know... I seen you do it. It's not lost."

Sam stopped and sat on the edge of his bed.

"You didn't lose it," Denny repeated. "It was moved. We don't know where or how or why. But we know who. We just know she moved it for a reason."

"We gotta go, Counts. Everybody's waiting." Sam began to relax. "Somehow, this is all working out the way it's supposed to."

Sam nodded and grabbed his bag. At the bottom of the stairs he dashed into the laundry room and gave his mother a quick peck on the cheek.

"Good luck!" she shouted. The back door slammed behind the boys.

Jessica carried a suitcase in each hand and walked into the kitchen. "I'm all ready, Mom." Ida Whitehawk looked up from packing bologna sandwiches into a woven basket.

"Can we stop at the Buildin' before we pick up Julia? I just want to talk to someone for a second."

Mike screeched to a stop next to the Appaloosa Express and Sam and Denny jumped out. As Sam started up the bus steps, he heard someone quietly call his name. He stopped and turned to his left. Denny glanced in the direction of Sam's gaze, turned back with a smile, and boarded the bus. Behind the Appaloosa Express stood Jessica.

"Hi," Jessica beamed.

"*Ta'c méeywi*[20]," Sam answered, although the morning was quickly slipping away. A few long seconds passed. "Are you going to Warm Springs pretty soon? It's a long drive." Then Sam added, "We have to go, like, now."

"I know." Jessica paused. "I just want to tell you, 'good luck'." She stepped closer toward Sam. He bent down to hear Jessica's whisper. "I have the knife." Their eyes locked. Then it happened. Jessica placed both hands on Sam's arms, stretched up, and kissed him. She twirled around and jumped into her mother's waiting car. Jessica turned back and waved.

Sam hurried onto the bus and ignored his teammates' complaints. He took a seat next to Denny.

"What's up with you, Counts?" A big grin spread across Sam's face. "Oh! Score, enit?!" Sam lobbed

---

[20] täts\ə\MĀ\wē

his duffel bag onto the pile of luggage that filled the last two seats of the bus and blocked the riders' views.

"I won't tell," Denny laughed.

Sam contemplated life as the old bus rumbled toward Oregon. Jessica. May. The knife. Denny was right. Events were in motion.

Earl Guerreros overestimated the Appaloosa Express's cruising speed. Even across the flattest stretches of the Lower Columbia Basin, they managed just 48 miles per hour.

Thirty-four miles west of Pendleton a wood-paneled station wagon passed them. Luggage filled every inch of the back. Three laughing high school girls made faces at the boys and waved. Jessica's little sisters crawled across Aunt Milly's lap in the front seat and mimicked their heroes.

Denny was gazing at the foothills of the Blue Mountains, thinking someday he would like to hunt there, when he noticed the girls in the passing car. He poked Sam and pointed to Vicky, Julia, and Jessica.

Sam saw Jessica search from window to window, and when she spotted Sam leaning across Denny to wave, their eyes lit up. As Jessica disappeared from view, Sam had one thought: "Me and Jessica. This is nice."

Silas Moses

The Nez Perce Nation boys' team arrived at the Warm Springs Community Center gym just as the pow-wow Grand Entry began. Seven drum groups beat the steady rhythm of an inter-tribal song. Dancers young and old slowly stepped to the drums' cadence behind an honor guard of Warm Springs war veterans.

Jessica and Julia entered the gym side-by-side. Their small feet skimmed the floor. Julia's and Jessica's serious expressions bore an understanding of their heritage. The girls didn't just know how to dance. They knew why they danced.

The long procession circled the gymnasium and became a spiral that filled the entire floor. Bells matched the heartbeat rhythm of the war drums. The drumbeat rose to a frenzy and climaxed with one thunderous downbeat. The dancers milled a few moments; a thousand small bells rang, until the public address system crackled.

"Ladies and gentlemen, my name is Silas Moses, and it is my pleasure to be your announcer for the First Annual Warm Springs High School Pow-Wow and Basketball Tournament! First off, I want to welcome the many Indi'n nations who honor us by being here today." Silas Moses paused for the crowd's appreciative response.

"We also extend a hand in friendship to our non-Indian visitors." Mr. Moses stopped. The host drum picked up the cue, striking a rapid series of drumbeats accompanied by high-pitched cries. The other drums joined in.

Mr. Moses continued. "We will send our dancers off the court and then introduce the many people who have made this event possible." The Grand Entry resumed, and gradually the queue of dancers exited the gym double-doors until only the drummers remained.

The dancers casually walked back into the gym and sat with friends and family. Silas Moses introduced the Nez Perce, Spokane, Kalispell, Kootenai, and Yakama drummers and then the two drums of the host Warm Springs tribe. Next, he paid tribute to the weekend's organizers and sponsors.

"Last, but not least, time to present the fine basketball teams here representing eight Indi'n nations. First the host team, the Warm Springs Renegades!" An enthusiastic cheer followed the announcement of each player's name. The introductions continued for the squads from the Shoshone-Bannock, Flathead, Spokane, Yakama, Makah, and Crow tribes.

As the Crow players stood, the boys grew still. "Man, those suckers are *tall*," Sonny spoke aloud what everyone was thinking.

"They look tough. Barely laughin' around, enit?" Jesse added.

"And now the team from the Nez Perce Nation."

Jesse, Sonny, Tony, Jimmy, Billy, and Junior stood. Terry sat frozen to his seat until Jesse reached under his arm and pulled him up. Jesse and Sonny nodded to their White teammates and gestured for them to stand.

Silence spread across the gym as the crowd stared at the half Indian/half white squad. Just then a wild cheer erupted from the upper corner of the bleachers behind the boys. They turned to see Jessica, Julia, and Vicky on their feet and yelling wildly. Behind them stood parents of the Lapwai players, also cheering their hearts out.

Laughter broke the awkward moment's tension. The Indian boys, including Terry, were introduced to polite applause from the crowd.

In a crowd that included members of tribes from across the West, the Lapwai boys had their own Indi'n Section.

59

As Friday night's dance competitions ended, the basketball players stayed in the stands. Soon, Silas Moses introduced them to their host families. Group by group the crowd dwindled. The Nez Perce Nation was the last team left. Moments later, they were down to the last four boys.

Sam almost didn't recognize his old friend. Gordy stood near the doorway, a head taller than his mother Beatrice and his auntie next to him. Aunt Milly beamed as she laced an arm through one of Gordy's.

"Redwing, you remember your old partner-in-crime, Gordy?" Seven years had passed since the last summer Gordy spent in Lapwai. Gordy's khaki-colored tribal police uniform made him look even older.

"What it is, Sammy. Staying out of trouble without me around?"

"Chize! Look at you! A policeman, just what you always wanted. Lookin' good."

"Yeah, I turn 18 soon, so they put me on. I'm gonna work this summer for the tribe then take criminal justice at Oregon State."

"Okay, we won't sneak out and steal Harold Miller's apples like we used to," joked Sam. As memories took Sam and Gordy back, the years fell away.

Gordy turned to the small group of onlookers.

"Lootz, right?" Luke nodded. "I thought so. I remember you guys. And Denny." Denny stuck out his hand for some skin.

"Gordy, this is Mike," Sam said. Gordy and Mike shook hands. "He moved to Lapwai this year, but he's a real sooyáapoo now, enit, Mike?" Mike smiled.

"Nice to meet you," he said.

Beatrice Roberts spoke up. "You four will be staying at our house." The boys thanked their host. "Aunt Milly thought it would be best this way," Beatrice added.

"Good call," thought Sam.

"Are you staying there, too, Auntie?" Sam asked.

"Of course. I have to keep an eye on you, make sure you're good boys. She hooked her free arm into Beatrice's. "Besides, me and my sister have a lot of catching up to do."

"So, let's get your stuff," Gordy concluded. The group headed toward the Appaloosa Express parked near the gym entrance.

Gordy signaled Sam to hold up. They let everyone go ahead a few steps. Gordy turned to

Sam as they stepped outside and whispered, "I found May's brother."

60

The Nez Perce Nation boys' team faced a tough day ahead.

The tournament committee tried to keep it simple the first year. Have a nice four team, two day deal, like a Christmas tournament. So they sent out posters to the nearby Yakama, Spokane, and Nez Perce reservations.

Well, the Flatheads heard about it and wanted in. Somehow, word spread south to the Sho-Bans at Fort Hall. They wanted some Indi'n time with other tribes, so <u>they</u> sent in their registration.

News travels fast in Indian Country. The Crows didn't care how far they had to drive, as long as they had a chance to beat somebody. The Makah just wanted someplace to go to get out of the rain. By now, the number of teams was totally out of control for a weekend tournament. There was only one thing to do. Play two games on Saturday.

The boys needed a good night's sleep.

61

Nez Perce Nation Boys' Team Versus Shoshone-Bannock Nation
Saturday, March 11, 1972

"In two years these Shoshone-Bannock boys are going to dominate those other A-4 teams down there in southern Idaho," thought Josiah Whitehawk. Seven sophomores and two freshmen made the trip to Warm Springs from Fort Hall. The talent was there. They were just no match right now for Sonny and Jesse and, well, everyone.

The Nez Perce Nation jumped out to an early 12 point lead. When the boys cleared out for the guards to go one-on-one, one jab-step or cross-over was all it took for easy lay-ins. Inside, Tony scored at-will. Shoot, he stood a half-foot taller than the young Sho-Bans.

They fizzled late in the first quarter. Coach Whitehawk called time-out and put Jimmy and Terry in at guards.

As it turned out, Terry didn't need to worry about playing in an all-Indian basketball tournament. Nobody wanted to see the young Sho-Bans humiliated. After all, Terry and the Fort Hall boys were the same age. Jesse and Sonny didn't expect to play much more this game.

"We're going to step back on defense, give 'em a coupla steps, let 'em shoot. We showed everybody enough for now. We'll just trade baskets with them," Coach Whitehawk directed. "Let's take time off the clock. Make five, six passes, then, if you're open, put it up."

"Tony, we'll pass inside, then kick it back out," Josiah Whitehawk continued. "We don't need to run up the score and renew bad blood with the Sho-Bans. We don't hunt buffalo much anymore, anyway. Besides, you might be in Fort Hall someday and run out of gas. You don't want all the Indi'ns there to recognize you and leave you standing by the side of the road."

The boys laughed and put their hands in the middle of the huddle. "On three, 'Pass'!" Coach Whitehawk called.

The four white boys reached in through their teammates. Sam, Luke, Denny, and Mike were glad to see the crowd get used to their team's 'unusual' configuration. They'd been stared at most of their lives anyway, hanging out with their Indian friends. As Jesse liked to say, "Hell with 'em if they can't take a joke."

The game slowed to the Sho-Ban's level and, just as Coach Whitehawk envisioned, the teams took turns scoring. Mid-fourth quarter, the young Fort Hall team wore out, and Lapwai's lead nosed up to 16.

It could've been a 40 point blowout, so when the buzzer sounded, the teams, including Lapwai's bench, passed each other in line with fist-taps and "Good game"s, and the Shoshone-Bannock boys walked off the court with their heads up, looking forward to coming back to Warm Springs for two more years.

The Nez Perce Nation's show of sportsmanship won the crowd's respect. They were going to need it for what was to come.

62

Aunt Milly locked the bedroom door behind her, pulled a small tin cup decorated with tiny blue camas pedals from an ancient corn husk bag, and placed it nearby. In a voice close to a prayer, she spoke.

"Do you remember this cup, May? You gave it to me so many years ago. I couldn't save you then, but I can help Jessica now." She closed her eyes and pictured May, and alongside her, Jessica.

"Her spirit is strong. You know it is. You've seen her with her sisters. She needs to use her power to protect the People. The power must be passed on." Milly paused.

"You're so caught up with what you lost, you don't see what you have. Not just me...you have others who carry memories of you. You will always be special to me. Nothing can change that."

"How do you want to be remembered, May?"

63

Nez Perce Nation Boys' Team Versus Warm Springs Nation

Miles and miles of high desert junipers separated the Warm Springs Renegades. Their reservation cut a wide swath across upper central Oregon, from the Cascade summits to the palisades of the Deschutes River.

Rough, spare country. Outdoor courts were often more lava rock than dirt. There was not much driving-to-town-for-pick-up-games on the Warms Springs Reservation. Plywood backboards nailed to four-by-four posts had to do. In fact, the Renegades were members of three separate, far-flung tribes: the Warm Springs, the Wasco, and the Northern Paiute. They often had to hone their basketball skills alone.

So they were shooters. All stood between five nine and six one. Against the Makah, they passed and passed and passed until someone got open. Bank. Swish. Whatever. They thumped Neah Bay by 17.

Saturday afternoon's game with Lapwai started the same way. The boys played tight man-to-man, had their hands up on shots, did everything right, but the Renegades got good, quick looks off simple high ball-screens and led by eight at half.

Warm Springs stayed hot and upped the lead to 12. Sonny and Jesse worked the clock for the last shot of the third quarter, and when Jesse found Tony on a back-door, the spread dipped to ten.

The teams traded baskets most of the fourth quarter, so when Sonny called time-out with three minutes left, the boys were still down by nine. In the huddle, they looked to Josiah Whitehawk for help.

"We can stop 'em, but it's going to take everything you got. And there won't be time to sub." The boys nodded in consent.

"We can't let 'em cross half-court and set up. You remember how to run your press?" They nodded. "Up front?" Jesse, Sonny, and Billy lifted their hands chest-high. "Top of the key?" Junior nodded. "Tony, you're at half-court for the long passes."

"Just like in Lewiston."

"Yep," Coach Whitehawk continued. "They can shoot, but not much else. They don't play as a team. I'm betting they don't know how to break a press."

Again, Josiah Whitehawk was right. The first three times Warm Springs brought the ball in, Jesse and Billy trapped the dribbler in the corner. On the Renegades fourth attempt to bring the ball down-court, Sonny picked off a wild toss back to the in-bounds passer. On the Renegades' fifth try, Tony saw the deep, desperate fling down-court all the way and easily out-jumped the shorter Renegade center to grab possession.

Each steal led to easy lay-ins on the Lapwai end. When the boys led for the first time in the game, Warm Springs called time-out with 26 seconds remained on the clock. The starting five rushed to the sideline to whoops and high-fives from the bench.

"Ten straight points! That's the way we used to do it in the old days. Way to go!" Coach Whitehawk said, hoisting himself from the bleacher seats. The boys gave him their full attention.

"They think we're going to keep doing what we're doing, so...you remember your half-court trap?" The boys again nodded. "We get the ball back, just hold onto it. Let the time run out. Here we go...hands in the middle." Josiah Whitehawk allowed himself a small grin at his newly-acquired modern lingo.

Warm Springs got the ball across mid-court, alright. This time, though, when the ball reached a Renegade spotting up in the corner, all he saw was a wall of Tony's and Jesse's arms, with nowhere to go. Time quickly ticked away, and the baseline referee called out, "Five seconds!" Lapwai ball.

Sonny brought the ball up, dribbling through the defense, and started to drive the lane, but instead pulled up at the foul line. Three, two, one second, and the game was over. A very tired but relieved Lapwai five walked off the court, gave Warm

Springs a yell, and shook hands with their opponents.

The boys thought of their third tournament championship game in four weeks as they headed to the showers, this time against the Crow Nation, easy victors over the Spokanes and the Yakamas.

All but one boy. Sam had something else on his mind. Gordy's words came back to him. "I found May's brother."

64

"There you have it, ladies and gentlemen," announced Silas Moses. "How about those boys?" The crowd cheered in support.

"Be here tomorrow. You don't want to miss the action, finishin' up with the big showdown between the Nez Perce boys and the Crow Nation from over to Montana!"

"Right now, we'll take about a half-hour, Indi'n Time, to get set up for a full night of dancin' from our young people. Don't go away... There's fry bread for sale out front by the pow-wow committee, and real soon young ladies' fast-and-fancy will get started."

The boys walked off-court to shower, take Silas Moses's advice on the fry bread, and find good seats to watch the girls dance.

At eight o'clock, the drummers began an inter-tribal entry song. Several dozen girls from tribes throughout western United States and Canada slowly entered the gym. Many girls danced side-by-side, their bells jingling louder and louder as the drumbeat tempo increased.

Julia and Jessica circled the gym, mirroring each other step for step, motion for motion. Their flowered shawls, flowing from outstretched arms, became wings. When Julia brushed the floor with one hand, the other high in the air, Jessica followed, two young hawks soaring on the wind. Soon, every eye was riveted on the brilliant Nez Perce dancers.

The girls neared center-court. Silas Moses, always the showman, gave the main entrance ticket taker, standing near the gym light switch, a downward hand motion. The gym suddenly turned pitch black. In a flash, the center-court spotlight found Julia and Jessica. The other dancers swirled in the shadows.

The drumbeats rose higher and higher. Still Julia and Jessica kept pace, their moccasins touching down for the briefest of moments, and then spinning into space. As if they could fly.

Faster and faster they danced, until they became blurs of color. All at once, with one thunderous downbeat, it was over. For a long moment, the gym was silent.

Seconds later, the crowd, now on their feet, erupted into high-pitched yells. All but one silent figure. High in the top row an elder looked out from under a large hat. Tears rolled down his shielded face, for he could swear he had just watched his sister, lost so many years ago, dance.

65

A sliver of moonlight hit Sam's watch. 12:00 AM. Midnight. He rose from the mattress on the basement floor of Gordy's house and tiptoed past his sleeping teammates. In the darkness he slipped on his pants, grabbed his shoes and "L" jacket, and crept up the steps to wake Gordy. Time to go get the girls. Then find May's brother.

The old friends ever-so-quietly slipped into Gordy's pickup. Gordy stepped on the clutch, shifted into neutral, and they coasted down the driveway. Crunching gravel was the night's only sound. Sam thought he saw a moving shadow in the living room cast by the corner streetlight, but the house remained darkened. Not until they were out of sight did Gordy turn the ignition key and drive away.

"We can explain everything in the morning," Gordy declared. "Right now it's up to us." Sam nodded.

Vicky was already waiting at the back bedroom window when Sam and Gordy rolled to a stop in the alley behind Edith Blackwolf's house. Her worried look stopped Sam cold. Jessica's pow-wow suitcase lay open on a chair in a corner of the bedroom...with one dress missing. "She's gone!" Vicky exclaimed.

Again.

Vicky slipped over the low windowsill into the breezy March evening and turned to help her best friend out the window. Julia rushed toward Sam. "We have to find her before..."

"I know where she went," Gordy interrupted. He slammed the window behind them, and the bedroom curtains stilled.

The girls eased. "You sure?" Julia asked.

Gordy nodded. "But háamt'ic! We gotta go outa town coupla miles, then up a dirt road."

Sam and Gordy hurried back to the pickup. Vicky and Julia crammed in beside them. Gordy cracked the driver's-side window to clear the windshield, already fogged in the crowded cab. They slowly drove out of town, scanning the dry arroyos on either side of the highway for their missing friend.

Just past a narrow concrete bridge over the Warm Springs River, Gordy turned onto a one-lane dirt road. The road forked, and Gordy stopped. He climbed out, lifted the top wire strand holding a rusty barbed wire gate in place, dragged it forward, and propped the post against a hedge of sagebrush.

As they followed a dry creek bed around a sharp bend, juniper branches brushing against the sides of the old pickup, its headlights spotted a slender girl walking slowly in the middle of the road. The moonlight cast a long shadow behind her. The outline of a small, darkened cabin stood in the distance.

Gordy parked in the middle of the weedy path. At the sound of the pickup, Jessica looked over her shoulder. Vicky and Julia got out and eased alongside her, and Sam and Gordy lingered behind. The girls each took hold of a cold hand. For the first time, Julia noticed the image of a bone-handle knife on her pow-wow dance companion's dress, beaded many, many years ago. Jessica glanced in both directions and gave her friends a brave smile.

"Don't worry. We're with you," Julia said. Jessica gratefully nodded. The boys headed back to the pickup.

Jessica stood frozen in place. "I...I don't need this..." she finally thought. "...I don't need her."

Like a bolt of lightning, it hit Jessica. "My friends will be there for me now whenever I need them. Will May?"

In the darkness of the pickup cab, the boys watched. "How did you know about this place?" Sam whispered.

"Took some work finding it, Sammy," Gordy answered. "Looks like nobody's been up here much for years. I knew this had to be it."

The five teens proceeded on foot. Past a cattle chute filled with tumbleweeds, they came to a two-room cabin. Wisps of wood smoke rose from a brick chimney. The girls advanced, with Sam and Gordy a few steps behind.

Jessica stepped forward and courageously knocked on a heavy pine-plank door. She waited, knocked again, and called, "Uncle. It's Edith Blackwolf's niece. Jessica." She took a deep breath. "I have something to give you."

A curtain parted. The lined face of an elderly woman peered out. Her silver hair contrasted with her smooth brown skin. She held an old pewter candlestick in one hand, a gnarled cane in the other. She opened the door. Inside, a wood stove glowed a warm red.

"Auntie. I hope we didn't scare you," Jessica spoke first. Her four companions stood several steps behind her.

"Oh, no, I don't get scared out here no more. I been livin' out here too long to get scared by some kids," the elder chuckled.

"Oh, I'm glad, Auntie. We won't keep you up. But we have something really important to give to Mr. Blackeagle. From someone long time ago. Is he home?"

Mrs. Blackeagle's face suddenly clouded. "No, he isn't here. But I'll take you to where he is." She stepped back inside the house, lifted an old quilt from a rocking chair by the woodstove, wrapped it around her shoulders, and stepped outside.

Gordy's police flashlight lit a worn path leading from the cabin. Mrs. Blackeagle laced an arm through Gordy's and ascended a small knoll. Several paces behind, Jessica clung to the leather sleeve of Sam's "L" coat. When the path veered right, they could see the moonlit outline of ancient gravestones, some marble, some wood. Gordy turned off his flashlight.

Mrs. Blackeagle unlatched an ornate iron cemetery gate, and they entered the graveyard. As Jessica's steps grew heavier and heavier, her grip tightened on Sam's arm for support. Just then it all became clear.

"My friends, and my family, are who I count on. They are all the protection I need... and I have myself." With that, Jessica finally let May go.

The power was now hers alone.

Jessica raised her eyes and approached a mound of freshly dug earth. The small group stopped.

"Arthur died three days ago," Mrs. Blackeagle explained. "He was sleepin' in his chair, next to a good, warm fire. I heard him singin' some of the old hymns in Indi'n, and I knew it was time. I covered him with that old blanket of his." Mrs. Blackeagle paused.

"My youngest son Marvin come out the next day, so we walked up here and picked out a good spot. Marvin dug all day. We wrapped Arthur the old way and laid him to rest."

Jessica stared at the grave. Through her tears she whispered, "We're too late. I wanted so much to help May give her knife back to her brother. That's all that mattered to me." Her voice faded in the darkness.

"You can, Granddaughter," came a voice behind her. Jessica stiffened. "Just turn around."

"Who...?" Jessica stammered and turned.

On the moonlight shadow's edge stood Josiah Whitehawk. With one hand holding his arm and another on her sister's, Aunt Milly gently smiled.

"May's *nipe*[21], Jessica," Josiah said. Their eyes met. "May's *younger* brother."

Jessica gasped and crumpled to the ground.

Jessica's friends rushed to her side. Vicky held Jessica's lifeless face in her hands. Sam reached for Jessica's left hand clenched in a tight fist. He unfolded her fingers and found the small, white knife.

He lifted it from Jessica's palm, and she opened her eyes. Sam guided her hand so she could place the knife down on a flat stone near Arthur's grave. Then he tenderly lifted Jessica off the ground. She tilted her head and gave Sam the faintest of smiles.

They followed Sam down the hillside path to the cabin. Julia opened the cabin door, Mrs. Blackeagle lit a kerosene lantern, and Sam lowered Jessica into Arthur's rocking chair near the wood stove. They watched Jessica's life return. She gazed around the room until her eyes found Josiah Whitehawk.

"Tell me again," she whispered.

---

[21] NĒ\pə

Josiah Whitehawk repeated himself. "Jessica, I am May's younger brother. When Mother and Father left us, our older brother Arthur went off to work. He sent us money. I was little, so May took care of me. When she got sick, I had to go to Lapwai, too."

"Just before they took us to the train station in The Dalles, I ran back to the house to grab one thing from home. The knife. It was on a small table," Josiah Whitehawk scanned the room. "Right over there." He pointed toward the bedroom.

Mrs. Blackeagle walked to a handmade pine table holding a propane stove and fixed Jessica a cup of hot tea.

"When May died, your great-grandparents came to the hospital. They told me, 'You're Aunt Suzie's grandson... She's not here to protect you, so we will,' and they took me in. They picked up May's few belongings." Josiah Whitehawk's voice softened and he smiled at Jessica. "Including that dress." Jessica smiled back and nodded.

"I became Josiah Whitehawk," he continued. "I found a new home. I haven't been back here 'til today."

Chize! Jessica's words after saving Sam at State came back to her: "Why me?" She had found her answer. May and she were family.

"Suzie...May...now me...the power of the protectors has come home," Jessica realized.

A few moments later, she watched Sam stir the ashes in the woodstove and place kindling on the glowing embers, and the fire burst into flames. Gordy walked outside and returned with an armload of firewood. The room remained very still but for the crackling fire.

"Mr. Whitehawk, did you know that Sam found the knife?" Vicky finally asked.

"Yes. I could see the signs. That knife has a lot of power."

Josiah stood, shuffled toward the woodstove, and added a piece of firewood. "I remember this stove. I had to go out and get wood in the snow." He smiled as his thoughts drifted to a distant time.

"Auntie, did you know Mr. Whitehawk was May's brother?" Sam asked.

"Of course, Redwing."

"Why didn't you tell Jessica?"

"She couldn't just return May's knife." Aunt Milly looked in turn at each of the young people. "You all helped bring it home." She smiled her thanks. "But only Jessica could return May's spirit, then let it go." Josiah nodded. "May can rest now."

No one spoke. Suddenly Jessica bolted upright.

"The knife! I can give you the knife now!" She reached into her empty pocket. Vicky touched Jessica's hand and explained everything that happened at the graveyard. Aunt Milly knelt at Jessica's side.

"May couldn't do it without you. As hard as it is to protect, it's harder to let go," whispered Aunt Milly. Jessica nodded. She knew.

"You did more than you know, Sayáq'ic húukux," Aunt Milly continued. "Now May's joyful spirit will protect her ancestors in the Afterworld from sadness. Once again she is complete."

"But the knife?!"

"It's with May's brother, Jessica."

"It should be with the one who gave it to her!" Jessica protested.

"It's in a good place, Granddaughter," Josiah Whitehawk assured her. "Besides..." He pulled out the knife he received after State. He turned it over and over in his hand and shined it on his pant leg. The room grew very still. "...I have a really good knife right here."

66

In a few moments, Gordy broke the silence. "Well, we better let everybody get some sleep. Coach Whitehawk has a big game tomorrow. We can't let the Crows off easy," he laughed. Soon, he was following his mother down the bumpy road from the cabin back to Warm Springs.

Gordy pulled up to the front steps of Edith Blackwolf's house. No need for secrets now. Gordy stayed in the pickup as everyone piled out. Sam and Jessica let Vicky and Julia go ahead.

"How do you feel now? Are you all right?" Sam looked down at Jessica.

"Okay, I guess. I don't know. I feel a little hollow, like I just let something go. When we left the knife, it's like I left a piece of myself." Jessica paused.

"I didn't realize how important the knife was to me. It was scary sometimes, but it was like May counted on me, and I couldn't let her down. I felt like I was helping every girl who couldn't go back home." Jessica brushed a tear from her eye. "I don't want to forget that I did that."

They stopped at the front door. Sam reached into his pocket and pulled out a small knife. "1972 State Champs" was engraved on one side.

"Maybe this will help." He took hold of Jessica's hand and placed the knife in it.

"Sam, no! This is yours. You won it at State!" Jessica said in astonishment. "You sure? Really?"

"Really. I want you to have it. Somehow, everything, the knife, State, May, you, everything would mean more to me if you had it."

Jessica turned toward Sam. "Qe'ciyéw'yew'." She placed both hands on Sam's shoulders and stretched up to kiss him. A long, long kiss.

"See you at the game, Counts!" Jessica laughed and went inside.

67

Sunday, March 12, 1972

The boys arrived an hour early to relax, dress down, and warm up. A stack of programs sat on a long table near the gym entrance where Earl Guerreros parked the Appaloosa Express. Each player grabbed one.

Jesse was first to notice. "Counts! Check this out! Your dream has come true! Even better than your Indi'n tie!" Sam's hand went to the beaded medallion Jessica gave him for Valentine's Day. "You're finally a real Indi'n!" The boys flipped through the pages featuring team rosters and remaining pow-wow dance contestants.

There, on page four, was the Nez Perce Nation team picture. Underneath, each player's name, height, grade, and tribe were listed. Next to Sam's, Denny's, Mike's, and Luke's names read, "Honorary Warm Springs."

Coach Whitehawk peered over Billy's shoulder. "Well, it looks like we got a full team now," he chuckled.

"They told me last night they were going to do this. They been watching you boys. They like the way you look out for each other. The Indian way." Mr. Whitehawk's voice wavered. "How you honored me by asking me to be your coach." Everyone gathered around him.

"When I told them you sooyáapoos went sweatin', then ate traditional food done the old way, it was settled." They turned toward Mike and laughed.

"I talked to the coach of the Crow team," Josiah Whitehawk continued. "They don't care who they play. They just want to play ball. If you four want to play today, you're in."

They looked around at their teammates. Billy broke the ice. "One last game... Let's take 'em to the hoop, enit?!"

68

Nez Perce Nation Boys' Team Versus Crow Nation

The championship game of the First Annual Warm Springs High School Pow-Wow and Basketball Tournament between the Nez Perce Nation and the Crow Nation was the greatest high school basketball game ever seen in Indian Country. The ball movement was exquisite. Jump shots, things of beauty. Fast breaks led to backboard-shaking dunks. Shot blocks weren't just clean, they were spectacular. No sloppy turnovers, no careless fouls. It was a perfect match-up between two great teams. It was magic.

Midway through the fourth quarter Silas Moses was so caught up in the action he missed putting several points on the scoreboard, so he simply turned the score off. He reached across the scorekeepers' table and closed the official statistics book, too. This one was for the pure joy of the game.

Some people say it was tied when the clock ran out. In the following weeks, the Lapwai boys swore they kept track of the score in their heads and won by two. Back in Montana, the Crow claimed a five point victory.

It didn't matter. It was every pick-up game the boys had ever played rolled into one sublime moment. It was their last game together. It was epic.

69

A huge crowd packed the Warm Springs Community Center gym for the pow-wow's last night. When Silas Moses announced the round dance, couples filled the court for one more chance to make memories. Jessica walked across the hardwood floor, head held high, straight toward the small group of Indian and white teammates and friends. She silently held out an outstretched hand for Sam to take. Sam stood and stepped between Sonny and Billy seated on the bottom bleacher seat, still holding Jessica's hand. They clasped hands and joined the other couples circling the gym.

Sam suddenly felt his partner's hands go cold. He looked down at the small figure beside him: a long shadow followed her.

"Are you staying here with your brother, May?"

She nodded.

"And Jessica goes home alone?"

Again, a brief nod.

"I'll tell Aunt Milly. She'll be happy."

"Qe'ciyéw'yew'," May responded in a whisper-voice as dry as cobwebs. "For everything."

The small hand in Sam's again felt soft and warm.

"'Eehé," Sam answered, still in-step to the beat of the war drum.

"'Eehé for what?" Jessica said in surprise.

"Oh! I meant to say, 'qe'ciyéw'yew'','" Sam stammered.

"Qe'ciyéw'yew' for what?"

"For asking me to dance."

Jessica smiled and squeezed Sam's hand. "Anytime, Redwing."

BIBLIOGRAPHY

Beall, Tom and R. D. Leeper. Legends of the Nez Perces. Lewiston, ID: Lewiston Tribune, 1931.

Slickpoo, Allen and Deward Walker. Noon Nee-Me-Poo (We the Nez Perces). Lapwai, ID: Nez Perce Tribe of Idaho. 1973

The Nez Perce Indian Joint Session of the Six United Presbyterian Churches. Nee Mi Putimt Ki Wanipt (Nez Perce Presbyterian Hymnbook). Caldwell, ID: The Caxton Printers, Ltd., 1967

National Tuberculosis Association Committee on Tuberculosis among the North American Indians. Tuberculosis among the North American Indians. Washington, D.C.: Government Printing Office, 1927

White Romero, Mary E. "Once There Was a Tuberculosis Sanitarium at Lapwai." The Golden Age Fall and Winter 2012: 32.

GLOSSARY

'Ácqa (ƏTS\kə): Male's younger brother

'Aláamtit (ē\LƏM\tit): Woman-crazy

'Eehé (a\HE): Yes (a response to "thank you")

'Ipéetes (Ē\pə\täs): Feather; the name of the Nez Perce's spring pow-wow

'Áyat (Ī\it): Girl

Chize: An interjection created by Lapwai High School students in the early 1970's

Enit (\E\nit): Slang; contraction for, "Ain't it?"

Háamt'ic (HƏM\tits): Hurry

Hóopop (HŌ\pōp): A dish made from pine moss

Lepít (lä\PIT): Two

Mitáat (mē\TÄT): Three

Náaqc (näks): One

Nén (nān): Older sister

Nípe (NĒ\pə): Female's younger brother

Qe'ciyéw'yew' (kəts\ē\YAU\yau): Thank you

Sayáq'ic húukux (so\YÄKH\its\hü\hük): Pretty Hair

Sooyáapoo (sü\ē\YAP\ō): Non-Indian

Ta'c halá p (täts\hə\LAUP): Good afternoon

Ta'c méeywi (täts\ə\MÄ\wē): Good morning

Ta'c kuleewit (täts\kə\LAU\it): Good evening

Te'lk k'úcwin (tə\LIL\ə\kwin): "Stick Indian" (a spirit)

Titóoqan (ti\TŌKH\in): Indian

Wewanekitpa himuna, wewanekitpa himunu: when the roll is called up yonder, when the roll is called up yonder (from *Nee Mi Putimt Ki Wanipt (Nez Perce Presbyterian Hymnbook)*)

Yú'c (yəts): Pitiful, poor; 'a poor thing'

The spelling of the **Pi-Nee-Waus** (*Place of Arrival*) Community Center and Café has remained unchanged since its construction in 1964. In Haruo Aoki's orthographic system, *Pi-Nee-Waus* is spelled *Páayniwaas*.

PRONUNCIATION GUIDE

\ə\   as in *but*

\a\   as in *ash*

\ā\   as in *ace*

\ä\   as in *mop*

\au\   as in *out*

\e\   as in *bet*

\ē\   as in *ease*

\i\   as in *hit*

\ī\   as in *ice*

\ō\   as in *go*

\ü\   as in *loot*

The Protectors Family Tree

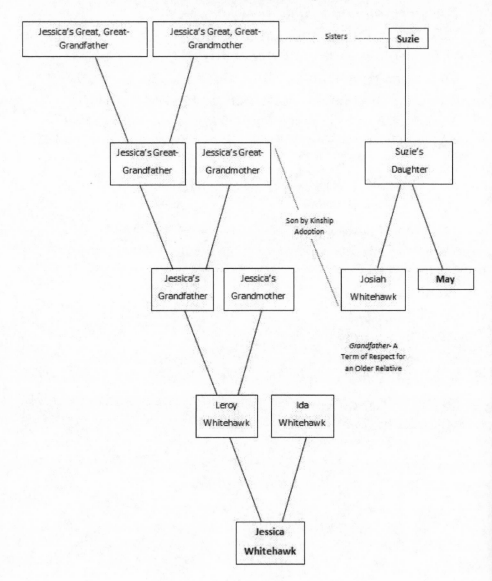

ACKNOWLEDGEMENTS

I want to give a special thanks to my wife, Betsy Wilson, for her constant support, idea-sharing, and encouragement. I could not have finished this project without her. Thank you, Allen "Lootz" Phillips for living this story alongside me and for helping me tell it. To my family: Claire, Andrew, and Elisa, thank you for letting me share this part of my life with you.

The many people who read my manuscript and offered their thoughts helped me so much: Gail Sipe, Madeline Buxton, Curt Wilson, Sandra Casanova, Niki Wolf, Barb and Doug Porter, Kathy and Steve Eckberg, Brian Wilson, Doug Nash, Caryn Lawton, Beth Deweese, Robert Clark, and David Scott.

I greatly appreciate the help of Angel Sobotta, Coordinator of the Nez Perce Language Program, Bob Caruthers of the Nez Perce National Historical Park, and Keith Peterson of the Idaho Historical Society during research for *Shadows Left Behind.*

PHOTOGRAPHS

Mylie Lawyer

Corbett Lawyer

Archie Lawyer (seated, middle)

The Lawyer (*Hallalhotsoot*)

Twisted Hair *(Walamottinin)*. Sculpture by Doug Hyde depicts Twisted Hair with Lewis and Clark, with The Lawyer at their feet. It is located at Lewis-Clark State College in Lewiston.

"Ant and Yellowjacket" Two Miles West of Spalding
"Rock formations of wind-shaped animal figures look down on May."

Celilo Falls on the Columbia River, Oregon, 1950's
"At Celilo Falls, her father, or an uncle, or one of her brothers glimpses a battered craft wedged between two boulders along the shore upriver."

Fort Lapwai Grounds

"When she first arrived at the Fort Lapwai Tuberculosis Sanatorium two months earlier on the train from The Dalles, May had told Milly that one of her grandmothers was Nez Perce."

Annie Yellow Bear near Kamiah, Idaho 1890

"Milly's oval face had reminded May of her sisters back home on the Warm Springs Reservation, digging roots on warm spring days on the prairie."

Nez Perce National Historical Park, Spalding Site
"Some of the stronger children rolled down the mill race banks and ran down the slough left from the days of the Spalding Mission."

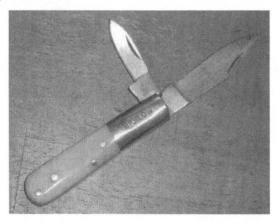

Bone Handle Two-Blade Barlow Pocketknife
"May was still thinking of home. She reached into her dress pocket and felt for a very special gift from her brother: a double blade Barlow knife."

Behind the Fort Lapwai Officers' Quarters, 2016
"May knew where they were: inside the long-abandoned canal that traversed the valley's western hills used to transport spring water to the village."

Sweat Lodge within a Wooden Shelter
"She (Milly) lifted a corner of a dark brown blanket the color of bark to reveal a tiny room."

Chemawa Indian School near Salem, Oregon, Early 1900s
"Four years later, she (Milly) earned a teaching certificate from Oregon State University and landed a position teaching home economics at an Indian girls' boarding school in Oregon."

"Carrying the Flag, Lawyer Arrives with the Nez Perces, May 24, 1855, at the Walla Walla Council" by Gustavus Sohon
"One time they used a thirty-four star American flag David's great, great-grandfather, The Lawyer, received before the first treaty as a tent."

The two remaining brick TB sanatorium dormitories are currently vacant and untended. This building housed Bureau of Indian Affairs offices after the sanatorium closed and is similar to the Lapwai Upper Elementary School building.

"The brick building at the base of the valley's western hills held the fourth, fifth, and sixth grades."

Nez Perce National Historical Park, Fort Lapwai Site

"She (Mrs. Preston) grew up nearby in the first floor apartment of a large house housed officers assigned to Fort Lapwai."

1972 *Kee-Mah-Mar*, Lapwai High School Yearbook
"Walking from the deep wooden, balcony seats of the Wildcat's Lair student section, down the hallway stairs to the locker room, they hear their town's applause."

The Nezpercians, A Jazz Band Comprised of Tribal Members, 1920's
"The Nezpercians had a gig that evening at the Pi-Nee-Waus Community Center."

Thunder Hill, One Mile North of Lapwai

"Yeah, well, Jesse and me and Luke were telling about how last year before football we ran down to Spalding to break in our new cleats, and we took the back road over Thunder Hill."

Photograph by the Author, 2016

"There's this one (cemetery) just up the road from my house on the hill where you turn to go up Soldiers Grade."

Waaya-Tonah-Toesits-Kahn (Blanket of the Sun)
"In summer he (Junior) rode broncs, following in the footsteps of his great, great-grandfather, the legendary Nez Perce cowboy Jackson Sundown."

Tony White Cloud, Jemez Pueblo, 1948
"For 20 minutes, in step with the rapid pounding of war-dance drums, He (Jimmy) wove himself through hoop after hoop, until seven interlocked into an intricate, dazzling pattern."

Nez Perce National Historical Park Collection

"The plant-dye colors of the corn husk bag draped over Aunt Milly's overstuffed chair had faded into soft pastels."

From the Author's Collection

"A photograph of turn-of-the-century Lapwai showed almost as many tepees as wood frame cabins."

The First Indian/White Integrated School District in the
Nation

"As the rickety old bus crept up the hill where Potlatch
Creek entered the Clearwater, the girls jumped out the
back door of the bus, ran to the top of the hill, and
waited there for the bus to finally arrive."

Fort Lapwai Tuberculosis Sanatorium
"She (Milly) handed Sam a large group photograph."

Lapwai High School Addition, 1942
"He (Mr. Barrett) loved the classic architecture of Lapwai High School."

Nez Perce Drummers, Grangeville Border Days
"For the Nez Perce, there was never a time before drums."

Nez Perce Veterans, Lewis-Clark Corps of Discovery
Anniversary Opening Ceremony

"The only sound was the faint cadence of the Nez Perce Veterans Color Guard, marching two abreast. "Left, left, left, right, left..."

On February 4, 1963 ice moved Spalding Bridge 12 inches off its foundation.

"As they crossed Spalding Bridge, Sam noticed the reflection from the last ice floes of the season backed behind the bridge piers."

9,393-Foot He Devil Peak (Center), Idaho

"She and Wolf waited for him on the crest of the Seven
Devils Mountains."

Lapwai Town Team, 1898

"Their town teams played spirited baseball games every
Fourth of July in the twenties and thirties until World
War Two."

Coyote Grade, Two Miles South of Spalding, 2016

"Háamt'ic, sooyáapoo!" Ron hollered to Justin as he got behind the wheel of his pickup to head back up Coyote Grade."

From the Bridge on Tom Beall Road, 2016

"Lapwai Creek had always been a companion."

Gaffed Salmon at Celilo Falls, 1937

"When she (Jessica) was ten, Grandfather taught her to gaff the Coho salmon making their way to the spawning grounds upstream."

Clearwater River (Left) Entering the Snake River at Lewiston, ID and Clarkston, WA

"For thousands of years, several confederated bands of the Nez Perce existed in the region where Idaho, Washington, and Oregon now meet, including areas around Lapwai, Kamiah, the Grand Ronde and Snake rivers confluence, and Tsceminicum."

The Spokane, Riparia, Washington, 1901
"Steamboats laden with newcomers chugged up the Columbia and Snake rivers from Portland, Oregon."

Nez Perce Encampment
"They visited family in nearby Lapwai often and maintained tribal ties at pow-wows and encampments."

Photograph by the Author, 2016

"The Appaloosa Express stopped in front of the Methodist Mission Church nine minutes later."

Stick Game, Sandpoint, Idaho, 1931

"She imagined her ancestors as teens, spending warm evenings flirting, while the older folks played stick games until the first light of dawn."

1930's Jingle Dress

"Folding the arms of her jingle dress into an ancient strap suitcase, she felt a hard lump in the waist pocket."

A Couple Round Dancing, Pendleton Roundup

"When Silas Moses announced the round dance, couples filled the court for one more chance to make memories."

**The 1970-1971 Lapwai (Idaho) High School
Basketball Team**
Back Row (Left to Right): Coach Rolly McNair, Sr.; Paul
Smith; Elisha "Gib" Scott; Dan Wilson, Jr.; Scott Wilson;
Rolly McNair, Jr.; Tom Webb, Jr.; Mike Greene
Front Row (Left to Right): Manager Steve Hyde; Allen
Phillips; Rick Taylor; Sid Armstrong; Tom Rickman, Jr.;
Kim Rickman; Manager Ken Huddleston

All photographs are by the author, from the
author's collection, or in the public domain, unless
otherwise noted.

28577322R00192

Made in the USA
San Bernardino, CA
07 March 2019